Vixen's

This was the last night she had of being a child. Tomorrow, another thing would begin.

It is Vixen's thirteenth birthday morning when her mother turns up unexpectedly. Vixen lives quite happily and calmly with her father. Her mother constantly travels the world, and Vixen very rarely sees her. This time, however, the surprise visit is only the beginning. It starts up a chain of events which lead Vixen to the most amazing discoveries.

Vixen has always loved foxes. When she was little she used to think she really was a fox. And all through her birthday summer, Vixen is haunted by the past, hunted by possible danger. But this time she can't run away.

FRANKIE CALVERT spent her childhood in Hornchurch, Essex; her teenage years in North Wales, and then came back south to do English and Drama at the West London Institute of Higher Education. After graduation, she wrote and acted with various theatre companies, including being half of a cabaret double-act. She has worked in several West End theatres in the varying roles of usherette, bar-tender, stage-door keeper, and Box Office clerk—all while continuing to write. *Vixen's Haunt* is her second novel.

ALSO BY FRANKIE CALVERT

The Sea Serpent

Vixen's Haunt

Frankie Calvert

OXFORD
UNIVERSITY PRESS

OXFORD

UNIVERSITY PRESS

Great Clarendon Street, Oxford OX2 6DP

Oxford University Press is a department of the University of Oxford.
It furthers the University's objective of excellence in research, scholarship,
and education by publishing worldwide in

Oxford New York

Athens Auckland Bangkok Bogotá Buenos Aires Calcutta
Cape Town Chennai Dar es Salaam Delhi Florence Hong Kong Istanbul
Karachi Kuala Lumpur Madrid Melbourne Mexico City Mumbai
Nairobi Paris São Paulo Singapore Taipei Tokyo Toronto Warsaw

and associated companies in Berlin Ibadan

Text copyright © Frankie Calvert 1999

The moral rights of the author have been asserted

First published in 1999

British Library Cataloguing in Publication Data available

ISBN 0 19 271807 X

Typeset by AFS Image Setters Ltd, Glasgow
Printed and bound in Great Britain by Biddles Ltd, Guildford and King's Lynn

ONE

When Victoria Courtney was a week-old, red-haired baby who wouldn't stop wriggling in spite of the August heat, her grandmother (who couldn't abide babies) had gruffly remarked:

'But she's like a little fox cub. She's a vixen changeling from the woods.'

Then she went away and never came back again.

In spite of her gruff tone, Vixen's father thought this was a charming and romantic thing to say—until he remembered that his mother-in-law had hunted foxes in her youth.

However, the name 'Vixen' had stuck. Apart from her looking like a fox, it was a feasible shortening of 'Victoria' and made a change from 'Vicky'.

Now, it was the same time of year some time later. In the yellow heat, Vixen was, with some trepidation, preparing for her thirteenth birthday . . .

The day before it, she was sitting out on Wandsworth Common with her friends, Rhona and Georgette. They were strung out across a shallow bank: Vixen at the top with her back against a tree; Georgette in her habitual hunched position halfway down; and Rhona stretched out full length at the bottom. The branches of the tree were sending out a dappled effect over the grass which the first two were caught in. Only Rhona was completely in the sun.

They were all exhausted. Up until then, they had been stuck with Georgette's eighteen-month-old niece. They had thought she would be collected within half an hour but it had taken Georgette's sister more like two

1

hours to turn up. Even then she was reluctant to take her child away again but Rhona had been firm. They had all watched, nearly in tears with relief, as the child, Livvy, was dragged away through the trees, kicking and screaming.

Vixen was the first of the three of them to be going into her teens. This was happening to her tomorrow.

'You won't feel any different,' said Rhona, stretching her arm out languidly in the heat.

'But thirteen's an unlucky number,' said Georgette worriedly.

Something white seemed to flit past Vixen's face. She turned her head sharply but, sun-dazed as she was, she couldn't be sure.

'What's the matter?' said Georgette.

'I thought I saw something,' said Vixen. Then: 'I don't think I want to be a teenager.'

'You don't get a choice,' said Rhona, drowning out Georgette's anxious 'why not?'. 'It happens to us all. I want a Cornetto.' She got to her feet.

They all made their way across to the hut that sold ice cream and Coke.

'Have you had anything for your birthday yet?' asked Rhona, expertly uncoiling the paper from her Cornetto.

'Some cards have come,' said Vixen, 'but I won't open them till tomorrow. And Auntie Margaret's made me a dress. I'm not allowed to wear it till tomorrow—so I haven't seen it yet.'

Georgette was concentrating hard on her ice-cream wrapper. She wasn't as deft at undoing it as Rhona was.

'Will you hear from your mum?' she asked Vixen, frowning as the paper stuck fast to the ice cream.

'Don't know,' said Vixen.

Rhona and Georgette exchanged looks.

'Doesn't she even remember your birthday?' asked Rhona abruptly. Georgette nudged her but she ignored it.

2

'Sometimes she does,' said Vixen. She pulled a strip of emerald-green paper off her ice cream and stared at it for a moment. Would her new dress be green too? She hoped so. She had dropped enough hints. 'And sometimes she doesn't,' she added about her mother.

There was a slight pause.

'But . . . ' began Georgette—but then yelped and jumped to one side to avoid a bounding dog. This caused a large blob of ice cream to fall off her cornet and land on its head. The dog looked very surprised for a moment at the coldness on its skull but obviously decided not to take it out on her. It bounded onwards.

Georgette was scared of dogs. Also spiders.

The three friends made their way back to where they were sprawled out before. This time, Vixen lay down full in the sun with Rhona, leaving only Georgette crouched in the half-shade. No one said anything for a few minutes. Vixen stretched and curled her limbs, feeling the sun twist over her relentlessly.

'This is bliss,' she said.

'It's even better if you keep still,' said Rhona drily.

Vixen immediately lay as if paralysed.

'Oh no,' she said. 'I can't keep that up.' She moved again. 'Who wants to come to the wild bit?'

'I don't,' said Rhona. 'Why can't we just stay here? You're acting all disturbed.'

'You'd be disturbed if you were thirteen tomorrow,' said Vixen.

'You're mad! It'll be much better being a teenager. I can't wait!'

Vixen didn't respond to that.

The three of them parted company about half an hour later.

'See you tomorrow,' said Rhona and Georgette—and Vixen went on her own to the 'wild part'.

There was a small pond there with yellowflag and

3

bullrushes. Vixen liked to sit by it and write things. She didn't have her notebook with her today but thought she would go anyway. As she was making her way through the high grass that surrounded it, she thought she saw somebody leaving it. It was like a flash of white T-shirt and a flash of white sock but nothing definite. Sun's in my eyes, she thought, rubbing them. But when she looked again, there was no one, coming or going, in any direction. However, by the side of the pond was a jam jar with a loop of dazzling white string round the rim of it—the newest-looking string Vixen had ever seen. Someone must have been here then, she thought. The jar didn't look as if it had been used though. It was dry and the string was too clean. Shrugging her shoulders, she decided to have a dip with it herself.

It was surprisingly absorbing—lying flat on the ground and dunking the jar into the pond. But suddenly she stiffened, with it half in and half out of the water. A familiar voice was shrieking through the bushes—that of Livvy, Georgette's niece.

I mustn't be caught like this, thought Vixen in a panic. I wouldn't put it past Georgette's sister to land her on me again even if Georgette's not here. Especially if she sees I've got 'something to play with'. She pulled the jar out of the pond, emptied it, and left it for the next curious fisher. Some vivid green weed had come up for her—who knew what would come next? And at least the jar looked used now. She fled. A second later, Livvy came crashing up—with her mother in hot and bothered pursuit.

Vixen was hot and bothered too on the way home. She felt ridiculously emotional—but she couldn't really work it out. When she got there, she found her father (whose name was Kevin Courtney) and Gregory, his friend, in the back garden. They were stamping down a patch of soil by the hundred-year-old wall. It looked very funny—two men in baggy shorts and big boots moving over a very small space, as if in a dance.

'What are you doing?' said Vixen.

'Mending the toilet,' said Gregory cheerfully.

Normally, she didn't mind his sarcasm but today she just wasn't in the mood.

'No need to be like that,' she said and, to her own horror, her voice cracked.

Gregory was taken aback.

'I'm sorry, Vix,' he said.

'We're compacting the soil,' explained her father quickly. 'I've just moved some plants from here and dug it over—and now we're compacting it.'

Vixen didn't say anything.

'Greg,' said her father, digging deep in his pocket for coins, 'go and get fish and chips. And beer. And a bit of cider for Vixen. She needs cheering up. She's thirteen tomorrow and doesn't want to be.'

'Oh I see,' said Gregory. 'Why's that then, Vixen?'

'Don't know, don't know,' mumbled Vixen. 'Things will change. I'm scared of it.'

There was a pause.

Gregory went to the chip shop.

Later, when Vixen was feeling better, everything was golden: the chips were, the fish in its batter was, the beer was, the cider was and, hanging over all of it, the evening sun was. They were sitting outside at the wooden table and benches. She and her father had salvaged them from a skip and then he had done them up. He was good at things like that. Their backs were against the section of wall that was covered in ivy so the leaves got caught in their hair and they looked like the Greek gods in Vixen's picture book that she had had for years.

Gregory went home not long afterwards.

'Happy birthday for tomorrow, Vixen,' he said,

kissing the top of her head and pushing a ten-pound note into her hand. 'Get some . . . oh, I don't know, pens and nice notebooks and things. That's what you like, isn't it?'

'Oh yes,' said Vixen. 'Thanks very much.'

She went and got her current notebook from her bedroom—it was a hard-backed one with foxes running through snow on the front of it—a Christmas present from Auntie Margaret. She was given lots of things like that—some she liked and some she didn't. There were times when she was obsessed with foxes—she dreamt of them and, when she was very young, she had sometimes believed she was one, disguised thinly as a human. She had always enjoyed running—but only for herself, not for the school or anything like that. That would have taken the foxiness out of it. All this had happened because her relations had made her into a 'Vixen' not a 'Vicky'.

She sat and wrote in the book while her father watered the garden around her. Gardening was another of his things. Vixen herself had a strange relationship with plants. She liked them and she liked being among them—especially when it was sunny—but she had no control over them like he had. She never felt like bending over the soil with metal tools in her hand. He could endlessly adjust them and trim them and nurture them and never get bored. Vixen had house plants in her bedroom that came and went. She quite often forgot to water them and then overdid it in an agony of guilt. If they died, she felt dreadful. She felt it was like murdering your children. Her father, on the other hand, was aware at any given time what state his plants were in—and which ones needed what. They were all over the house, reaching effortlessly for the light, luscious, green, and cultivated.

This was the last night she had of being a 'child'. Tomorrow, another thing would begin.

Two

The next morning, Vixen was dragged out of the kind of dream she hadn't had for years. There were foxes in it and some sort of chase—but before it got really tough, the door-knocker thumped right into it and woke her up. She sat up, startled, hair all over the place, and then thought to look at her watch. It was seven o'clock. Who, in their right mind, would call at that time?

Her mother would.

Vixen's bedroom was at the front of the flat. She clambered dizzily out of bed and opened the curtains very slightly. Her mother was standing on the doorstep, waiting to be let in. Here she was again after an eighteen-month gap, as unannounced as usual. Even that quick glimpse unearthed the usual curious feelings Vixen had about her—and they were nothing like people might expect.

She went into the hall in her long T-shirt and nothing on her feet and opened the front door.

'Hello, Vixen,' said her mother and smiled briefly.

'Hello,' said Vixen. 'Come in.'

They didn't embrace or anything—they never did. They both walked through to the kitchen. Vixen automatically did 'morning' things; she unlocked the back door, opened the window, and took the kettle to the tap.

'Happy birthday,' said her mother simply. She was carrying a rucksack on her back which she now took off and opened. She extracted a small, hard parcel from it and handed it to Vixen.

'Thank you,' said Vixen. 'I'll open it in a minute.'

She put it on the table. The parcel was round and

started to roll so she wedged it between the fruit bowl and a letter rack. 'Tea or coffee?'

'Yes please.'

'Which?'

'Oh . . . tea, please.'

'Sit down.'

'I can't stay long.'

(She never could.)

She did sit down though which was a relief to Vixen. There was such a restless, haunted atmosphere that always hung about her mother. She always looked as if she would be off any minute. It was easier when she was sitting down.

I'm thirteen today and the first person I see is my mum, thought Vixen. Not necessarily what she would have expected. She took her in with sidelong glances as she was making the tea.

Here she was in the kitchen, Vixen's mother, Laura Thomas: thirty-five years old; quite tall; long face; brown hair tied back, as usual, in a low ponytail; hazel eyes that never looked fully at you because they were always surveying the distance over your shoulder; very tanned—but just in passing—not because she lay down in the sun and waited for it; dressed in jeans, blue T-shirt, and big brown boots. Vixen's father wore similar boots—they were urban and trendy on him—but the ones on her mother's feet would be seeing a lot of mud and rough terrain. It was strange; you probably couldn't take too much of her—not that Vixen ever got the chance to find out—but you couldn't hate her either. Even if she was your mother and she had left you. She was too troubled and active for that. What Vixen felt for her could probably be described as 'awe'. She didn't really understand it.

She took the teapot to the table and sat down opposite her.

Silence for a couple of minutes.

'So, have you got a plane to catch?' asked Vixen eventually.

'Yes,' said Laura.

(She always had.)

'Where are you going?'

'Ghana.'

'You've been there before, haven't you?'

'Oh yes.'

'So . . . so have you got friends there?'

'There are people I know.'

'Will you be staying with them?'

'Sort of. I'll be working in a hospital.'

Vixen was surprised at that. She had only had the vaguest idea what her mother actually did apart from going to places. At one time, it had been writing articles for travel magazines—none of which Vixen or her father had ever read. Now, suddenly, for the first time, Vixen felt a pang about that. She also realized that she had asked her mother more questions now, on the morning of her thirteenth birthday, than she ever had before.

Laura looked at her watch. 'I must go,' she said and stood up. 'Thank you for the tea.' She swung the rucksack round in one deft movement and got it on to her shoulders again.

Vixen automatically went ahead of her into the hall. She opened the front door and the sunlight blasted in at them. Vixen recoiled from it slightly because it was the most intense it had been yet—but Laura just strode unflinchingly into it. The front garden sloped down below street level. As her mother was ascending the steps that would take her up to the pavement, Vixen was thinking, unaccountably, of Joan of Arc. They had 'done' Joan of Arc in history last term. It alarmed her that she was thinking of her now. But perhaps it was just

9

because the sun was so intense, it was like fire. And her mother was going into it . . .

A woman in a print dress was walking past just as Laura stepped on to the pavement. More people were coming up behind and there was a man in a denim shirt in front. Vixen always thought that climbing out of their front garden on to the street was like coming out of another world.

She went back inside and through to the kitchen. But she had only been there a moment before she had a sudden desire to check how far her mother had got. How strange! She went back out into the front garden, climbed the steps, and looked up the street. Laura was nearly at the top by now and a small figure in white shorts was gliding behind her as if following her although this wasn't likely. He must have come up out of one of the other gardens, thought Vixen vaguely. Gone on an errand for an adult perhaps . . . a pint of milk, a newspaper. She went back in.

The next thing that happened was her father's bedroom door opening and he came into the kitchen in his dressing gown, yawning.

'You're up early!' he said.

'That's because Mum came,' said Vixen. 'Didn't you hear the knock on the door?'

'No,' he said, startled. 'What time was that?'

'Seven o'clock.'

'How long did she stay?'

'About half an hour.'

'Oh.'

Pause.

'How is she?'

'Fine. I think.'

'Good.'

Another pause.

10

'Oh . . . oh . . . Happy birthday,' said Kevin, remembering priorities. 'What's this?'

He had lighted on the hard, round parcel on the table, lodged between the fruit bowl and the letter rack.

'My birthday present from Mum,' said Vixen. 'I forgot about it! I should have opened it when she was here!'

Her father held it out to her.

It was wrapped in thick green tissue paper—but not sellotaped. She unravelled it to reveal a little tin globe, very neatly made.

'Oh,' said her father as if he didn't know what to think. 'Er . . . do you like it?'

'I do,' said Vixen, rolling it from hand to hand.

'Does she . . . does she think that you'd like to travel too?'

'Don't know.'

The telephone rang. Her father thankfully answered it.

'That was Margaret,' he said. 'She'll be here in about an hour.'

That was how the day would be: relays of visitations—although the first one had been unexpected.

Auntie Margaret arrived with something wrapped in silver paper. Vixen was secretly apprehensive: it seemed ungrateful but what sort of dress would her aunt have produced? Auntie Margaret had trouble believing that young people genuinely liked what they wore and tended to think that she knew better.

Vixen opened the parcel very slowly while her aunt and her father watched in embarrassing anticipation. She was quite taken aback to find herself holding a garment that was completely white. So it was the same colour as yesterday's Cornetto after all—but like the ice cream, not the green wrapping paper.

'Er . . . thank you,' she said warily. She didn't know if

she dared unfold it in case it had frills like a bridesmaid's dress.

'Well go and try it on then!' said Auntie Margaret enthusiastically.

Vixen slunk off to her bedroom. She closed her eyes when she first shook the dress out—then opened them very slowly. She went weak with relief. The dress was utterly simple. No frills, nothing offensive. Not the colour she would have chosen but at least it wasn't pink or peach. She re-emerged into the living room with it on.

'There now!' said Auntie Margaret with satisfaction. 'I do like to see a young girl in white.'

'You haven't worn all white since you were an angel in the school nativity play!' said Kevin.

'I wasn't an angel,' said Vixen. 'I was the Holy Ghost.'

On that note, they moved to the room where the kettle was.

'Now . . . have you got some nice shoes to wear with it, Vixen?' said Auntie Margaret to her barefoot niece.

'We're getting her some boots today,' answered Kevin.

'Boots! What do you mean "boots"! Why don't young girls wear girls' shoes any more?'

'Because we don't like them,' said Vixen.

'But . . .'

Her father cut in here.

'Margaret,' he said. 'It's Vixen's thirteenth birthday and if she wants a pair of boots, she shall have them. And anyway, she wants to look the same as her friends do. Remember all the hell we went through as kids because our parents wouldn't let us!'

Auntie Margaret looked rather taken aback by this. She obviously hadn't thought of it that way.

There was a pause.

'Toast?' asked Kevin pleasantly. 'Marmite?'

'And the dress is lovely,' put in Vixen.

Auntie Margaret stayed for breakfast. Vixen was interested to note that she cut her toast and Marmite into 'soldiers' like she used to for her sons when they were babies. Maybe she took comfort from this.

After Auntie Margaret left, Kevin and Vixen walked to Clapham Junction where they bought boots for Vixen. That was her father's present to her. She also spent the money Gregory had given her on two new hard-backed notebooks (not with foxes on—one had just patterns and the other had an intricate picture of a haunted house) and a stack of pens. Then they charged back with their carrier bags banging against their legs because Kevin's parents were due at half-past one and these particular visitors were always early.

Sure enough, they were waiting outside the front door as Kevin and Vixen came plunging down the steps of their front garden.

'Steady on, steady on!' cried Vixen's grandad, putting out a hand to stop her.

'Sorry we're late!' said Kevin, gasping for breath and trying to get the key in the lock. 'We've been shopping.' And they all crowded into the tiny hall.

Nana, as expected and like Auntie Margaret, was very unsure about Vixen's boots.

Vixen had decided, quite a while ago, not to care what Nana said about clothes. As far as she could gather, everyone else's grandmothers were the same—except for one of Rhona's who was Jamaican and laid-back and a jazzy dresser herself.

Vixen's dad, even at thirty-five, wasn't free of being criticized either. Having gathered that it was taboo to make derogatory remarks about Vixen's choice of footwear on her thirteenth birthday, Nana started on him instead.

'I just don't understand,' she said, 'why you men these days wear those big boots and socks with your shorts. Why don't you get some nice sandals like your father's?'

Vixen and her dad giggled over the image of him in sandals like Grandad's—but Nana started to look stern so they subsided.

'Different generations like different things, Mum,' said Kevin good-naturedly. He was never ruffled by remarks about clothes. He was confident enough about what he looked like.

But the next subject she touched on did ruffle him.

'Are you taking Vixen on holiday this summer, Kevin?' she suddenly asked.

He put his mug down and started fiddling with a teaspoon.

'Er . . . I haven't got any plans to,' he said. 'I've been too busy at work.' He plunged the teaspoon in the mug.

'You've already stirred that, Kevin.'

He stopped, rather moodily.

Holidays were a bit of an issue for Kevin Courtney—ever since the disastrous wholesale travelling he had done with his wife when they realized that he didn't like it and that she didn't want to do anything else. It seemed to have put him off for life. He and Vixen did go away sometimes—but not usually for more than a weekend and not as often as some people did.

'When does Vixen go back to school?' asked Nana.

'Not for a few weeks,' mumbled Kevin.

'Then there's still time to—'

'Oh, I won't be able to go away now!' he said, half in panic and half guiltily—because of Vixen. 'There's a controversial play starting at the theatre—they won't be able to spare me.'

Nana raised her eyebrows.

'And why not?' she said.

'Because I'm the Box Office manager.'

Nana stopped—but then dived in again after a very short break:

'But Vixen ought to have a summer holiday,' she said. 'We'll see what we can do.'

'What's controversial about the play?' asked Vixen.

'Oh, don't worry about that, dear,' said Nana quickly.

'Don't be silly, Mum,' said Kevin. 'Of course she should know.'

'Is it about drugs?' said Vixen. 'Or is it about . . . ?'

'Any more tea, anyone?' put in Nana very brightly and busily.

Kevin winked at Vixen.

'I'll tell you later,' he said.

Just before her grandparents left, Rhona and Georgette arrived. Vixen opened the door to them. The first thing she did was anxiously scan the whole front garden in case Georgette's niece was lurking somewhere. But no, they weren't to be saddled with her today. Vixen sighed with relief. She was also satisfied to see that both Rhona and Georgette were wearing dresses with boots so Nana could see it wasn't just her being a freak. Vixen's dad greeted them and then went off to make pizzas. Rhona and Georgette were fascinated by him doing this because he made them completely himself—even the dough for the bases.

'Everyone else I know buys frozen ones,' said Rhona.

'Or orders them from a takeaway,' said Georgette.

They were always fascinated by the flat too because it was so tiny.

'It's like stepping into an old canal boat,' said Rhona, who had been on a canal holiday last year.

Kevin laughed—and started chopping olives. Vixen saw Georgette gazing anxiously at them.

'Don't you like olives?' she asked.

15

Georgette could never answer with a straight 'yes' or 'no'.

'I'm really sorry,' she said, 'but . . . '

'Georgette doesn't like olives,' said Vixen.

'I won't put any on hers then,' said Kevin.

Vixen steered her two friends into the garden and they sprawled out under the apple tree. Evening was starting—and the sun sank down into the walled garden so it was like lying in a bowl of warm, gold soup. An apple thudded down from the tree missing Georgette's head by an inch.

'It would have been just your luck if it had hit you, George,' said Rhona and twirled the apple round by its stem. It had a maggot-hole so it couldn't be eaten.

'My mum came this morning,' said Vixen.

'Did she?' said the other two eagerly.

'Was she on the way anywhere?'

'What was she wearing?'

'Did she stay for long?'

'Did she come because it was your birthday or was it a coincidence?'

'Did she bring you anything?'

'Yes,' said Vixen. She got up, went into the kitchen, picked up her present and came out again.

'Leave the door open,' her father said. 'I'm boiling to death.'

The smell of tomatoes and onions wafted out after her.

'Brilliant,' said Rhona. 'I'm starving.'

Georgette looked worried. She wasn't sure if she liked pizzas at all—it wasn't just the olives.

'My mum bought me this,' said Vixen, and put the tin globe down on the grass in front of them. There were four or five apples scattered there too, and the globe was a similar size. The effect was very strange—as if the world had shrunk and fallen among the discarded fruit.

'It's pretty,' said Georgette.

'What a funny present!' said Rhona.

Vixen started rolling the globe and the apples about like marbles.

'I still don't want to be thirteen,' she said warily.

'Oh, don't be so—' began Rhona.

Then Vixen's dad called from the kitchen and distracted them.

THREE

A couple of weeks later, on a Saturday, Vixen called round to see Auntie Margaret, who lived two streets away. Auntie Margaret opened the door and was very pleased to see her.

'Someone to go shopping with,' she said.

The door of the sitting room was ajar and Vixen could hear some sort of sport buzzing and whizzing on the television. She could see three pairs of legs—one pair very long—stretched out over the carpet. Her uncle (Ray) and two cousins (Robin and Mark) were arm-chaired and completely absorbed.

'You're lucky,' said Auntie Margaret. 'Your dad isn't interested in sport, is he?'

Vixen giggled. The last programme she had seen her father absorbed in was *Victorian Kitchen* when the woman showed you how to get stubborn jellies out of moulds without having to melt the edges. She and her dad had then raked through the junk shops in Clapham Junction to find exotic moulds of their own—and ended up with a rabbit and several strange geometrical compositions. They had eaten shapely jelly until they were sick of it.

'Vixen and I are going to the market!' Auntie Margaret called into the sitting room and then went through the front door really quickly.

'Otherwise they start asking me to get things,' she explained to Vixen, 'and we'd have to go to boring bicycle shops or something.'

They strolled past the houses down to Balham High Street, Auntie Margaret giving marks out of ten to everyone's front gardens on the way.

'They ought to cut that bush back,' she said, and 'Isn't it time they mowed that lawn?'

Vixen glazed over at all this and only jerked awake when her aunt said, 'So what's your dad doing about a summer holiday?'

'Oh, don't you start,' mumbled Vixen—and went into 'automatic pilot' speech. 'Dad's "Very Busy At Work" and Nana and Grandad are "Seeing What They Can Do".'

'Does that mean you'll be going away with them?'

'Don't know. Don't think so.'

Much as she liked them, she sincerely hoped not.

'But—'

'Look at that nice stone window box,' interrupted Vixen before this could lead into criticism of her dad which made her uncomfortable.

'Yes, but it's a bit messy, isn't it?' said Auntie Margaret. 'They should . . . ' and Vixen happily glazed over again.

Balham market was full of the usual assortment of vegetables, cheap candles, and cleaning stuff. Auntie Margaret started sifting through a heap of shiny avocados and Vixen was idly glancing at them too when she heard a commotion from the stall behind. She turned round and saw a man with his hands full of plantains and garlic, arguing with a stall-holder. Then the stall next to it caught her eye and her attention was arrested because it was the cheap toy stall and today it had goods she hadn't seen there before. Brightly-coloured wooden things were hanging on strings, and she made her way towards them.

They were puppets—crudely-made objects without joints in their legs so you could only jump them up and down, not make them walk properly. They were garishly, not finely, painted—mainly animals: dogs and cats, cows and donkeys. Vixen looked, as she always did, for a fox but there wasn't one.

'Have a go with one, love,' said the man behind the stall and dangled a cow at her. 'They're only £3.99.'

She took the cow half-heartedly, jiggled it up and down for a few seconds and handed it back. The man looked expectantly at her but she just smiled and moved on. Something stopped her from getting very far though. There was a scuffle and a pattering of feet behind her, accompanied by a single, high-pitched laugh—like an odd chord in the bustle of the market. Vixen spun round and saw the puppet man looking straight at her. Whoever had run past his stall was presumably somewhere up among the back boxes of lettuces by now. There was a puppet all in a heap in front of the man as if someone had just dropped it there. He picked it up and flourished it.

'So there was a fox,' said Vixen impulsively—but the man didn't answer. She took a closer look at the fox-puppet he was operating. It was much more supple and better-made than the others had been. He was making it run round in circles and then stop and turn its head very realistically. Vixen could almost have believed the nose twitched. The fox wasn't red though, it was white.

'Is it an Arctic fox?' asked Vixen, determined to get some speech out of him. But he didn't answer. It was as if he didn't hear.

'Is that one more expensive than the others?' she demanded.

The man still didn't answer—just carried on manipulating the fox. It was starting to give Vixen the creeps.

'Why don't you answer?' she said.

The man suddenly gave the strings a lurch and the fox sank to the floor, nose down and front legs out flat. Vixen didn't wait to see any more. She walked back to the avocado stall.

Auntie Margaret had bought two avocados.

'I need tomatoes now,' she said, 'and—' She stopped and looked at Vixen. 'Are you all right?' she said. 'You look all ruffled.'

'Er . . . yes. Yes thank you,' said Vixen.

'Time for a break,' said Auntie Margaret and led her into a café on the corner of the market street.

'This was the only thing that ever made shopping bearable for Robin and Mark,' she said, and ordered tea and crusty rolls. When they bit into the rolls, the crumbs flew out like miniature sandstorms on to their plates.

'Thank you, Auntie Margaret,' said Vixen.

'That's all right,' said Auntie Margaret, draining the last of her muddy tea.

'Junk shops now?' said Vixen eagerly. 'To see if we can find some bargains?'

Auntie Margaret wrinkled her nose.

'I'm not keen on all that,' she said. 'Not like your dad is. I'd rather have everything new.'

Vixen got her to one though—where she found a nice old saucer with a fox on it.

'But it's no good without a cup, is it?' said Auntie Margaret.

''Course it is,' said Vixen but not so that the shopkeeper could hear her. To him she said, 'Will you let me have this for fifty pence please because the cup's missing?' (The saucer was marked a pound.)

The shopkeeper looked at her sharply but she didn't flinch.

'Seventy-five pence,' he said reluctantly.

Vixen handed it over.

'You're your father's daughter,' said Auntie Margaret, as they were leaving the shop.

'Well of course I am,' said Vixen who never saw the point of statements like that. She knew Auntie Margaret would be far more reluctant to say 'you're your mother's

21

daughter' but she suspected it could be relevant at times. Or maybe she was nothing like either of them. Who could tell?

FOUR

Something unheard-of happened the next day. Vixen's mother rang to speak to her—and it was only two weeks since her last contact. It was usually more like two years between sightings.

'Are you in England?' asked Vixen in amazement.

'Yes.'

'That was a short trip!'

'Yes. We got the work done very quickly.'

'Aren't you going straight off somewhere else then?'

'Not immediately. I wanted to see you first.'

Vixen took this in slowly.

'Are you still there?' said her mother.

'Er . . . yes.'

'Will you meet me in Soho for lunch?'

'In Chinatown?'

'Yes.' (Laura never suggested English food.)

'All right then.'

'Do you know where the Brown Bear pub is?'

'Yes.'

'I'll see you outside there at two o'clock.'

'Right.'

Vixen had been in Chinatown with her mother once before, and several times with other people, but she remembered the time with her mother most. More than anyone else, Laura made it seem like a twisting, mysterious maze with dragons raised up in odd places and noodles always bubbling in cauldrons. Vixen didn't know how she did it but the same thing happened again this second time. It was probably part of the general haunted intensity that always clung about her mother.

This time, as Vixen was approaching the meeting place (outside the Brown Bear), her mother didn't notice until she was right on top of her. Vixen actually stopped and studied her from a short distance: Laura was leaning against the wall of the pub, staring downwards. She was in her jeans and short denim jacket with a small rucksack over one shoulder. The expression on her face was so troubled that Vixen was shaken. She moved up to her very slowly.

'Hello, Mum,' she said.

Laura looked up.

'Vixen,' she said and smiled—at least, her mouth turned up at the corners but there was still a hunted look in her eyes.

Vixen fiddled with her buttons, feeling awkward.

'Are you hungry?' said Laura.

'Starving.'

'So am I.'

She immediately started striding off, knowing exactly which restaurant would do. Vixen had to half-run to keep up. They went at a rapid pace, passing all the big, bright, flashy places and going under golden archways until they came to ground in a side street and went through a doorway so narrow that it was almost like a plank in the wall rather than a door. The restaurant was tiny—and no other customers were there. There were only three tables and a small counter with a big bowl of oranges on it. An elderly Chinese man came forward, smiling.

'Hello,' said Laura. 'Anywhere?'

Vixen thought this was a funny question to ask because there were only three tables anyway and all exactly the same. But she supposed it was etiquette.

The man nodded and they established themselves in a corner.

'Is this your favourite restaurant?' asked Vixen.

'It's the most authentic,' said Laura.

Well, she should know, thought Vixen. She's been to China.

'Do you like most things? Shall I order?' said Laura.

'But we haven't even looked at the menus yet.'

'There aren't any menus here.'

'Oh. Well . . . go on then, you order,' said Vixen, beginning to panic a bit. Did 'authentic' mean not much choice and strange gut-things coiled on plates?

Laura smiled at the waiter and he came over to their table, without a notepad and without a pen.

Vixen listened fascinated while she reeled off a long list of things. Lots of fish was included which she was pleased about and at least three different kinds of mushroom. The man then disappeared briefly.

'How will he remember all that without writing it down?' asked Vixen in awe.

'He just will,' said Laura casually. Then: 'Are you all right with chopsticks?'

Vixen felt panic rise again. 'I always try them . . . '

'Good.'

'But usually end up using a fork,' she finished lamely.

Laura laughed.

'Well, you won't be able to here,' she said. 'They haven't got any.'

Vixen was terrified.

She needn't have worried though; when the food came, it tasted so startlingly good, it was like a firework display in her mouth. After a few dramatic seconds, she didn't think about what she was doing with the chopsticks—they were just the instruments that were assisting her. She completely relaxed. She and her mum started talking and about halfway through the feast she was aware of a real joy in the occasion. This had never really happened between the two of them before.

'Do you know what you want to do?' asked Laura, expertly hooking some squid on to her chopstick. Unlike a lot of adults, she didn't add 'when you grow up' but Vixen knew what she meant.

She answered immediately: 'I want to be a writer.'

'Really?' said Laura—then added absently, 'I used to do a bit of writing. Not books though. Articles for magazines. To make money.'

Vixen nodded, wishing she'd read some of them.

'I thought you might want to run,' continued Laura. 'You were always running when you were a child.'

Vixen was tempted to say 'How do you know, you weren't there', but didn't because that would have spoilt the atmosphere. She was also quite surprised at the statement. To her, running was simply part of being a fox—not something she would want to do professionally.

When they asked for the bill, the man glided to them with it on a plate. In his other hand was a larger plate with slices of orange on it.

'Thank you,' said Laura and Vixen.

He smiled.

Laura went to pull a leather wallet out of her pocket. It wouldn't come at first so she tugged it harder. As it hit the air, a photograph fell out of it to the floor. Vixen scrabbled for it immediately but then hesitated, thinking maybe her mum didn't want her to see it. She looked up.

'Well pick it up then,' said Laura pleasantly.

Vixen picked it up and looked at it.

'Was this taken in Ghana?' she asked.

'Yes.'

'Just last week?'

'Yes.'

It was a picture of a group of people, mostly African, two English-looking, leaning on spades and smiling at the camera. It looked as if they had been digging trenches—there was a real feel of mud and sweat and good humour about the shot. The two English people were Laura and another woman who looked about the same age. They both had their hair tied back with bright, patterned scraps of material. Vixen was amused to note that the second woman had an African baby in her arms for the photograph but that Laura was doggedly hanging on to her spade. There weren't many people who could get her mother to hold a baby!

Vixen handed the photograph back. It was a nice picture. She thought her mother looked nice in it—more happy and relaxed than she usually did. Everyone in the group was smiling—even the baby.

They thanked the waiter and left, running their tongues over their teeth to dislodge the shreds of orange.

'It's been dead good,' Vixen was starting to say, 'thank—'

'You don't have to go yet, do you?' interrupted Laura.

Vixen was taken aback.

'I don't,' she said. 'But you do, don't you?'

After all, she usually did.

'No,' said Laura. 'Not quite yet. Let's walk for a bit.'

Incredulously. Vixen fell into step beside her.

When she got home that evening, her dad looked at her in surprise.

'You were a long time,' he said. 'Did you enjoy it?'

'Oh yes,' said Vixen. 'We went to a tiny Chinese restaurant and the food was so good, I forgot I'm not good with chopsticks and then we walked through the . . . ' She tailed off because Kevin was looking at her oddly.

There was a silence.

Vixen felt unbelievably awkward.

'I ought to take you out more,' he said.

They both blushed.

He seemed to be thinking quickly.

'I'm on an early the day after tomorrow,' he said. 'Do you want to meet me at work and we'll . . . we'll go to a film or something?'

'All right then,' said Vixen. 'That'll be good.'

FIVE

Two days later, at five to six in the evening, Vixen emerged from the tube straight into the whirl of Piccadilly Circus. Her dad worked at the Seraph Theatre which was right in the middle of it. Vixen gazed up at the statue of Eros for a moment because she liked it, then entered the theatre with the sound of the fountain behind her. It mixed in quite oddly with the roar and scream of the traffic.

The Box Office was a tiny, closed-in den to the left of the main door. There were two windows let into it; her dad was sitting at one of them on the inside and Gregory, who was the Theatre Manager, was leaning in from the outside, talking.

'Hello,' said Vixen.

Gregory, who, until she spoke, had been a headless man in a black suit, pulled his head out of the hatch and became himself again.

'Hello, Vixen,' he said.

'Hello, Vixen!' echoed her dad from the innards of the den.

'You looked like a headless ghost,' said Vixen cheerfully to Gregory.

'Well . . . funny you should say that . . . ' he said.

Vixen felt the hairs prick up on the back of her neck.

'Why?' she asked.

'Because the theatre ghost's been sighted again. One of the cleaners saw it this morning.'

'Thought he saw it,' put in Kevin.

There was a pause.

'Come into the auditorium with me now and let's see if we can see anything,' said Gregory.

29

'Oh I don't know,' said Vixen.

She was torn between fear and mad curiosity.

'Go on, Vixen,' said her dad easily. 'You won't see anything.'

'You saw it once!' retorted Gregory.

'Thought I saw it,' corrected Kevin.

'You never told me, Dad!' cried Vixen.

'I didn't want to scare you. You were only about six.'

'But now you're a teenager . . . ' said Gregory.

'Only just!' said Vixen.

But fascination won. She padded across the foyer after him.

The whole of the auditorium was underground. It was famous for it. Every night, the wooden barrier was pulled back and you went down the stairs even if you had tickets for the Upper Circle. Some people got very confused. There were coloured tiles with patterns and lettering all the way down the stairs. Even though she had seen them before, Vixen looked at each panel carefully to prolong the minutes before she might see a ghost.

'They're all names of composers,' said Gregory, slipping automatically into his 'we're on a theatre tour' voice. 'When this was first built, it was to be a concert hall, not a theatre.'

Vixen looked at him fearfully.

'Is it one of them that's the ghost then?' she asked. 'Were they all so annoyed that their stuff wasn't played here after all that one of them haunts it?'

Gregory laughed.

'Nice idea,' he said. 'But these are all men. Our ghost's a woman. She always sits in the middle of the front row of the Stalls and gazes up at the stage.'

'Was she in love with one of the actors?'

'The story is that one of them was her son. But he didn't know. And she couldn't tell him.'

'Why not?'

'Nobody knows.'

Pause.

'What does she look like?'

'Well, you might see for yourself, mightn't you?' said Gregory mischievously.

Vixen shuddered—but she still followed him.

They turned through a door on the Dress Circle level and were immediately plunged into the curious stillness and coolness of an empty auditorium. The door shut itself tight behind them and the smell of the velvet seats wafted up. Vixen found her voice lowering automatically even though no play was in progress and no one else was there.

'What time does the play start tonight?' she whispered.

'Half-past seven,' said Gregory in his normal voice which startled her. It seemed to boom rudely around the hushed, enclosed space.

Vixen was standing with her back to the stage.

'I'm sure the pink wallpaper is very interesting,' said Gregory, 'but it's not usually where the ghost hangs out.'

Vixen laughed at that. Rhona said 'hangs out' a lot— but if you applied it to a ghost, it could mean something completely different. Her heart gave a sudden lurch when she imagined the ghost floating against the wall, feet off the ground.

'Come down to the front,' said Gregory and paddled in the deep carpet down to the front of the Dress Circle. Vixen followed, a foot or two behind.

He grabbed hold of the pink velvet padding on the front ledge and leaned over. Very slowly, she did too.

She stared down to the middle of the first row of the Stalls, her heart beating hard. But there was nothing there. She screwed her eyes up, remembering that

31

sometimes you can catch things like that—misty shapes of things that aren't available to the full gaze. But still nothing.

'Er . . . can you see her?' she asked Gregory.

'No. Looks like she's moved on for now.'

Vixen would have expected to feel relieved—but she wasn't. She was strangely disappointed instead. Gregory looked rather crestfallen too. Vixen suspected he had been let down by the ghost many times. They made their way in silence back to the foyer.

Her dad was speaking on the telephone and running his fingers expertly over the computer keyboard finding the date the caller wanted to book tickets for.

Vixen went to the Box Office window to ask him how long he'd be.

She now noticed that the other member of staff today was Stephanie who worked mainly in the central phone room but occasionally 'covered' in the Box Offices. This would be awkward for Kevin because he had gone out with her briefly and then they stopped. Vixen never knew who finished with whom—but she was well aware that today Stephanie was very firmly reading a magazine.

'Hello, Stephanie,' said Vixen.

Stephanie glanced up, flushed from her intensive reading. Then she saw who it was and her face relaxed.

'Hello, Vixen,' she said.

They had liked each other—which made it quite easy for Kevin. Vixen had detested the girlfriend he had before. She had never really rowed with her dad before that time, but when he was going out with Marie (even the name was silly, thought Vixen), she had packed up a discarded rucksack of her mother's all ready to run away and try and live with Auntie Margaret or Nana (neither of them ever knew this plan of hers). But before she was quite ready to do it, Marie had tried to pressurize her dad into going on a three-week foreign holiday—and he had backed off, terrified. So Vixen and he got on again. Sometimes Vixen felt guilty when she thought about it, but she couldn't help it; she hadn't liked the woman.

Kevin finished the booking and dashed his fingers dramatically over the keyboard to signal the end. Then he stood up and got his jacket on.

'It's a bit hot for that, isn't it?' said Vixen.

'Oh . . . er, yes,' he said and took it off again—all in a fluster presumably because of Stephanie. She, on the other hand, neatly sidled into his seat with the minimum of fuss and applied herself to the computer. This was the nearer window—the one all the customers saw first.

'Oh . . . right. Thank you, Stephanie,' said Kevin—and lingered awkwardly.

'Come on, Dad,' said Vixen. 'We'll miss the beginning of the film. Bye, Stephanie!'

'Goodbye, Vixen, goodbye, Kevin,' said Stephanie calmly.

Gregory was now on duty in his dinner suit, addressing the usherettes in the auditorium.

Kevin's choice of film was an old black and white French one with sub-titles showing at the Salamander Picture House. Rhona would have called it 'arty-farty'; Georgette would have said it was 'boring and old-fashioned'; and Vixen had a moment of panic as she and her dad were taking their seats. I should be seeing something big and trendy and American, she thought, so that I can talk to my friends about it. But from the moment the music started and the first credits crackled on to the screen, she was captivated.

It was a long film. Three hours later, it was a real shock to leave the darkened auditorium and black and white pictures and plunge back into the coloured world again. Vixen even felt sad about it.

'Did you like the film?' asked her dad, discreetly wiping away a tear of his own.

'Oh yes,' said Vixen. 'Thank you, Dad.'

She was in a trance.

When they got home that night, she got out her hard-backed notebook (She had finished the one with foxes on. Now it was the haunted house one that she had bought with the money Gregory gave her.) and wrote a lot.

'Still the same story?' asked Kevin.

'Yes. It's a novel.'

'When do you think you'll finish it?' he asked with interest.

'Don't know. Soon. Maybe tonight . . . ' she looked up at him with feverish excitement. 'That film really inspired me.'

He smiled.

'Aren't you afraid of plagiarizing though?' he asked later.

She froze in mid sentence.

'What does that mean?'

'Copying. Maybe without realizing. But you might find everything you've written tonight is taken straight from the film.'

Vixen thought for a moment, then laid down her pen and closed up the book. She felt suddenly grumpy—and looked it.

'Oh, I didn't mean to put you off!' cried Kevin in alarm. 'Keep writing!'

It was midnight before he could persuade her to open the book again—then he had the embarrassment of informing her that she really ought to be in bed.

'You've got Rhona and Georgette coming tomorrow, haven't you?' he said, trying to soften the blow.

'Oh, yes. Good,' said Vixen and went slowly to bed.

She didn't turn her lamp off though. She put her

floating dressing gown on over her nightshirt and heaped all the pillows up behind her on the bed. She didn't lie down—she half sat, half reclined. She and her dad called this the 'suffering Victorian heroine' pose. Like that, for tonight, she sat and wrote. It was far too hot for the dressing gown but to take it off would spoil the effect. Instead, she took the duvet out of its cover, flung it on the floor, and just used the cover on its own.

Two hours later, there was a knock on her bedroom door. She started violently.

'Er . . . come in,' she croaked. She didn't know why her throat felt sore—it was as if she had been saying the words of her book out loud instead of writing them down.

Her dad walked in. Well, who else was there? But, just for a moment, Vixen had wondered . . .

She gazed at him.

'Good night, Vixen,' said Kevin gently and turned off the lamp. 'See you in the morning.'

He left the room.

Vixen considered the risk of turning the lamp on again and continuing. But, instead, she felt the pen and notebook slip floorwards from her hands where they landed with a soft thud on the discarded duvet—all humped up like a cream-coloured beast. She lay back and closed her eyes.

But her head was in too much of a whirl to let her sleep. Conflicting things were at work in there; images from the film she had seen and the things she had just written in her novel. Or were they conflicting? Maybe she had 'plagiarized' and they were the same—which wouldn't do . . .

Racked by not knowing, she finally fell into an uneasy sleep and her dream was vivid:

It began in a field.

She was in the field.

But she wasn't Vixen Courtney, a thirteen-year-old girl with red hair—she was a real vixen. She felt her tail wave and her ears prick up on top of her head. There were other foxes there too, all grouped about as if it were a party. She counted them rather obsessively, checking several times over, and it came to twelve other foxes—thirteen including her. And thirteen, of course, was a dodgy number. And it was the age she hadn't wanted to be.

She wasn't sure about one of the twelve—he looked as if he were made of wood, not flesh and fur—and he was white, not red. However, the other foxes seemed to accept him much more readily than they did her.

'You're not a real fox,' they were communicating (she wasn't sure how they did it; whether they actually spoke or did it some other way). 'You're not a real fox. You've plagiarized, you've plagiarized . . . '

Then she realized there was a booth set up at one end of the field so she went closer to investigate. Her dad was in there selling tickets. There was a big sign outside announcing 'FOX HUNT. GET YOUR TICKETS HERE'. Vixen was horrified. Did that mean that she and the twelve other foxes were going to be pursued by baying dogs and people with strangled accents on horseback?

The dream then seemed to rush forward in time and she was on the run. She couldn't actually see the hunters but she could hear them calling to each other in posh voices and the horses' hooves thundering and the dogs running . . . it all seemed to be a long way behind but very audible. And then out of the trees, immediately in front of her, stepped her mother. Vixen skidded to a dramatic halt. Completely matter-of-factly, her mother scooped her up and put her into the rucksack she always had. Then she put it on her back.

'Dad was selling the tickets!' cried Vixen, heartbroken.

'That's his job,' replied Laura simply.

'But it was tickets for the fox hunt—and I'm one of the foxes!'

'He probably didn't realize.'

The noises from the pursuers had now disappeared.

And then the dream had changed. Vixen was human again, walking next to her mother in the unknown wood. A little way ahead of them was a boy in white who kept turning round and beckoning to them with a strange smile on his face. He didn't appear to be walking particularly quickly but no matter how much they speeded up themselves, they couldn't catch him up.

SIX

She woke up not long after this and didn't give herself any time to adjust. She got out of bed at once and staggered into the kitchen. Her father was so startled, he jumped up from his chair.

'What's the matter?' he cried.

'I had a nightmare! I was a real vixen in a fox hunt and you . . . and you . . . '

He pushed a chair under her and she collapsed on to it.

'What was I doing?' he demanded.

'You were . . . you were . . . '

He tried to help:

'Were chasing you on a horse?'

'No, you were in a box office selling the tickets for it.'

There was a horrible silence.

Vixen shuddered but then was still. Quite slowly, Kevin walked round the table and sat down opposite her.

'Vixen, it was only a dream,' he said seriously.

Another silence.

'What . . . what time are Rhona and Georgette coming today?' he asked.

Vixen sighed with relief.

'Oh yes,' she said croakily. 'They're coming, aren't they? Good.'

Kevin quietly sawed two slices of bread off the loaf and slid them into the toaster. He pushed the butter dish and the little brown pot of Marmite towards her as if they were gold and frankincense.

'Thank you,' she said.

'Don't think any more about the dream.'

He left for work an hour or so later, and Rhona appeared not long after that, her black hair all oiled and scraped back into a tight knot on the back of her head.

'Has your auntie been?' asked Vixen.

Rhona nodded. Her aunt always liked to do her hair in severe styles. They suited her though.

'Let's put your hair up too,' said Rhona.

'All right, but let lots of tendrils hang out and leave me plenty of fringe. I don't suit "severe" like you do.'

They had just finished the hairdressing operations and Vixen had more grips in her hair than she would have believed possible when the doorbell sounded again.

'Good. It's Georgette,' said Rhona and they both went to answer the door, proudly tilting their decorated heads.

But, to their horror, Georgette was not alone. She was holding the hand of her eighteen-month-old niece.

'Why have you brought her?' asked Vixen.

'Oh, I know it's a pain,' said Georgette fretfully, 'but my sister's come round to see my mum and she wants a break from her again.'

'But why should we be stuck with her?' demanded Rhona.

Georgette looked ready to cry.

'My mum said I was being selfish if I didn't help,' she said.

'That's all very well,' said Rhona. 'But you had a . . . had a . . . '

'Prior social engagement,' assisted Vixen.

'Exactly—one of those,' said Rhona. 'And there's no reason why Vixen and me should look after your sister's kid even if your mum thinks you should.'

'Shall I take her away then?' said Georgette, bitterly disappointed. 'I could take her on the common, I suppose. I'll leave you both to it.'

She stifled a sob.

'No, no,' said Vixen heavily. 'Come in. We'll just have to make the best of it.'

Georgette didn't need telling twice. She bundled the child into the flat at once.

Unfortunately, she let go of her hand rather quickly— and Kevin and Vixen did not have a very child-friendly flat. It was full of 'objects of interest' which Vixen liked to collect and her father to arrange—and some of them were placed at low levels. The first thing the little girl did was reach for a carved elephant. She knocked it over and one of the tusks fell out.

'Livvy, don't touch!' cried Georgette.

'It's a bit late to say that now!' said Rhona. 'Vixen's dad will go mad.'

Georgette bit her lip in horror but Vixen said, 'No he won't, he's not like that.'

She picked up the elephant and put the tusk back in. It promptly fell out again.

'Glue,' said Rhona. 'Have you got any?'

'I should think so,' said Vixen. 'I'll—'

Then they were distracted by Livvy's inquisitive little fingers closing round the rim of a bowl of pot-pourri.

For some reason it made Vixen cling even tighter to the elephant. Rhona and Georgette both made a rush to save the pot-pourri but it was too late. Over the bowl went. The flower-dust flew up in their faces; the rug was a mass of crackly petals. Georgette went down on her knees and started to shovel it back in the bowl, bright red in the face and saying, 'I'm sorry, I'm sorry.' Livvy, meanwhile, had sauntered off at toddler-pace to fiddle with the controls on the television and try and pull the plug out. Rhona made a grab for her and lifted her up, whereupon she kicked and screamed.

'Georgette,' said Rhona in a dangerous voice.

'Yes?' said Georgette, terrified.

'Have you nearly finished picking up that pot-pourri?'

'Yes. That's the last bit.'

'Sit down then.'

Not daring to argue, Georgette sat down on a stiff-backed chair.

'Keep your niece there!' said Rhona and plonked her on her knee.

Georgette automatically put her arms round Livvy but, in such an interesting living room, Livvy didn't want to be clamped down in a sitting position. She wriggled and squirmed and struggled, yelling lustily.

Vixen shouted across at Rhona over the din:

'Let's try the garden!'

She finally put the elephant down in a much higher place than it was in before and led the exodus into the garden. Georgette followed her, hanging on to Livvy with difficulty. After a couple of seconds, Livvy slithered out of her arms altogether, like a slippery fish. Rhona, bringing up the rear, had a face of grim determination. She swooped down and hoisted the toddler into the air again. Georgette resignedly held out her arms but Rhona had had enough.

'This is how you do it,' she said—and slung the child over her shoulder.

'Oh, be careful, you'll drop her!' cried Georgette.

'You mean, like you just did!' said Rhona.

Livvy wasn't a slippery fish now; she was the rock of Gibraltar. She had a surprised look frozen on her face which lasted until Rhona set her down in the garden. Then she immediately smashed a snail with her little fist and tried to eat a stone.

'What had that snail done to you, Livvy?' asked Vixen sorrowfully but Georgette was saying, 'Never mind that, she'll swallow the stone!' and made frantic efforts to get it out of her mouth. She managed it finally, gave her a stick to play with instead and Livvy instantly stuck it hard in her own bare foot. They all watched in awe while she drew the inevitable breath—then the shuddering wails began.

'Suppose she's really hurt her foot?' said Georgette, but they looked at it carefully and there wasn't a mark.

'Let's just ignore her and try and have a conversation. That might work,' said Rhona.

'You . . . er . . . you start then,' said Georgette, still with her eye nervously on Livvy.

'Did you know that . . . ' began Rhona. But Livvy, having finished wailing, started chanting 'Mummy, Mummy, Mummy . . . ' so loudly that it was impossible to speak over her.

'She wants her mum, you'd better take her home!' Vixen shouted at Georgette.

Georgette mumbled something in reply but Livvy was still going 'Mummy, Mummy, Mummy!'

'Can't hear you!' bawled Vixen.

By the most tremendous effort, Georgette raised her voice. Shouting didn't come easily to her.

'Her mum won't be there now,' she said. 'She and my mum have gone shopping.'

Livvy stopped then, exhausted for the moment. There was a heavy silence from all four of them. Vixen was racking her brains trying to remember what she liked doing—or having done to her—when she was eighteen months old.

Livvy was raising another stone to her mouth. Vixen knocked it out of her hand, picked her up like Rhona had, and slung her on to her back. She started being a 'horse' going round and round the garden.

'Oh good, she likes that,' said Georgette with relief.

Vixen was a horse for several minutes but unfortunately with these things, the person doing them gets sick of it a lot quicker than the person receiving them. Livvy was demanding 'More, more . . . ' and

Vixen wanted to just stick her in a tree, tell her she was a bird sitting on an egg, and leave her there.

'Enough now,' she said and put her right under the garden table, thinking it would give them a few seconds' grace while she crawled out again. She flopped down next to the other two on the grass. Georgette was looking at her in an awed sort of way and Rhona looked wryly amused.

'Shall we . . . er . . . begin our time now?' said Vixen. But they were already glancing at the table expecting to see a determined little figure coming out from underneath it to disturb them.

She didn't though. They actually managed to exchange about five sentences between them.

'Is Livvy all right under there?' said Rhona, trying to sound totally unconcerned.

'We'd know if she wasn't,' said Vixen, and they exchanged a few more sentences.

Then Rhona stuck her head under the table.

'Oh, brilliant!' she said and emerged with her eyes shining.

Vixen and Georgette looked at her expectantly.

'She's asleep,' she said simply.

They all gave muffled cheers.

'Right!' said Vixen and got up to get provisions.

While she was in the kitchen, she had another idea. She went to get something out of the cupboard under the stairs and raided another cupboard in the living room for a piece of cardboard and thick marker pen.

She took these things into the garden first. In the cupboard under the stairs had been an old fireguard which she now set up in front of the garden table so it looked like a cage.

'We should have done that in the first place!' said Rhona and laughed.

'What are you doing, Vixen?' asked Georgette, sounding terribly worried again.

'It's all right, George, it's only a joke,' said Vixen. 'Just while she's asleep. There's a notice too.' And she fixed the piece of cardboard on the front of the fireguard with sellotape. 'FOR SALE' it read.

'Child for sale, child for sale,' chanted Rhona.

'Is that funny?' asked Georgette doubtfully.

''Course it is, it's hilarious,' said Rhona. 'Relax, George. Vixen's already said it's only a joke.'

Then they sprawled, picnicking, in front of the cage.

They were deep in a conversation about what they imagined for their futures when there was a knock on the front door.

'Is that your dad home from work?' asked Georgette.

'He's not due for ages yet,' said Vixen. 'And anyway, he's got a key.'

She got up, brushed grass off her shorts and T-shirt, and went through the flat to open the front door.

It was her mother.

'I don't believe it!' cried Vixen, truly astounded. 'You're here again!'

She was seeing her more times this summer than she would have believed possible.

'Hello,' said her mother.

'Oh hello, hello,' said Vixen, realizing she should have said that to begin with. But then she burst out with, 'Don't you go away any more then?'

'Yes,' said Laura. 'But I . . . er . . . '

'Come in,' said Vixen. 'Rhona and Georgette are here.'

Laura smiled faintly. She had never met them before. Once again, that overwhelming troubled air was hanging over her. Vixen had a real wave of sadness for a moment. It cast a shadow over the bright day.

'Would you . . . like some tea?' she asked. 'And . . . and to meet Rhona and Georgette?'

Her mother nodded. She followed Vixen into the kitchen; they both paused while the kettle was seen to and then both walked into the garden.

'Rhona and Georgette,' said Vixen. 'This is my mother.'

She said 'mother' rather than 'mum'. It seemed more appropriate.

'Hello,' said Rhona at once, sounding very interested indeed.

Georgette's greeting was a shyer echo of that. Both she and Rhona stopped sprawling and sat up straight.

'Would you like a tuna fish sandwich?' asked Rhona, holding out the plate.

Vixen cringed slightly, expecting it to be too 'English' for Laura—but Laura actually smiled and said 'Thank you very much.' She took one and bit into it at once.

Vixen was staring at her.

'Is that all right?' she asked incredulously.

Laura looked surprised and stopped eating.

'Of course,' she said. 'Why wouldn't it be?'

Vixen realized that she had never before seen her mother eat a tuna fish sandwich—only Chinese noodles and vindaloo and tagliatelli in restaurants.

Everything was going quite well—and then, suddenly, Laura noticed the 'cage'.

'What's in there?' she asked. 'What's for sale? Is it rabbits or something?'

'Something like that,' said Rhona, deadpan.

'Have a look,' said Vixen and drew back the fireguard with the 'FOR SALE' notice on it. Laughing, all prepared to join in a joke, Laura bent down to look under the table . . .

Abruptly, she straightened. Her face had gone deathly pale. Vixen had never actually seen anyone's face do that before—she had thought it was just a dramatic device used in books. Now she knew it really happened. Her mother swung round on her in a way that was entirely new.

'What made you think of that, Vixen?' she demanded.

Vixen was dumbfounded.

Laura's voice went up a notch.

'I said, what made you think of it? It's not funny at all!'

Vixen got a bit angry then. Who was her mother to come here and start shouting at her? She had hardly seen her since she was a year old!

'It's a joke!' she cried. 'Just a joke!'

'Oh shhhhh!' said Georgette nervously. 'You'll wake Livvy!'

Vixen rounded on her next. There can be few people who don't feel annoyed by being shushed.

'You shouldn't have brought her anyway!' she said. 'You don't come and visit friends and bring other people's babies with you without asking!'

Georgette burst into tears; Vixen stopped abruptly, feeling terrible, and Rhona made an amused comment about real vixens and tempers.

'She wasn't called Vixen because of temper,' said Laura in an odd, strained voice. 'It was because she looked like a fox cub.'

'Is that a compliment?' asked Rhona, laughing. She was obviously trying to lighten the atmosphere and Vixen was grateful, but Laura's face was like a tragic Italian madonna's in a painting. A good painting, too, so you didn't feel impatient with it; you felt overawed. Never in her life had Vixen seen a face so desperately sad.

'I must go now,' said Laura—and turned and left. Vixen didn't feel inclined to show her to the door—she just felt like howling, although that would be more wolf-like than fox-like.

'Er . . . doesn't your mum like jokes?' asked Rhona, and even she sounded shaken now.

'I don't know, I don't know!' said Vixen, very agitated. 'Don't forget I hardly know her really!'

Then she said, 'I'm sorry I shouted at you, George.'

'It's all right.'

There was a pause.

They tried to get back to 'normal' after that but it was very difficult. Livvy woke up about half an hour later, droopy-eyed and fretful.

'I think my mum and sister will be back now,' said Georgette hastily, and whisked her away—or dragged her rather. Livvy wasn't awake enough to be whisked.

Rhona then had to get back to see her aunt before she left, so Vixen was on her own now, mooching about the house and garden, hair-grips coming out at every turn, and not knowing what to do. She couldn't settle to reading or writing, usually two of the things she was most passionate about. Running, she thought. I'll have to run. But it was too hot for that really. She dithered a bit longer and then started to make herself leave for the common. Just as she was about to put her hand on the front door, someone thumped the knocker. She nearly jumped out of her skin—but she knew, before she opened the door, that it would be her mother again.

'Hello,' said Laura, meeting her gaze directly. 'I'm very sorry about earlier on.'

'That's all right,' said Vixen, flustered.

A front lock of hair had climbed out of its metal clutches and was hanging down over her eye. Laura made a movement with her hand—then seemed to change her mind. Vixen was amazed: had she imagined it or had her mother nearly moved her hair out of the way for her?

But she didn't do things like that!

Laura sighed. 'Are you hungry?' she asked.

'Yes,' said Vixen. 'Starving.'

She was quite surprised that she was—then realized

47

that not one of the tuna fish sandwiches had passed her lips that lunch time. There had been too much distraction.

Laura turned round and started to climb back out of the front garden. Silently, Vixen followed her. They didn't need to confer as to where they were going. There were two restaurants down the road: one was a tea-room that did poached eggs on toast and fruit cake and endless tea in china pots—and the other was a curry house. They walked into the latter.

This meal was nothing like as joyful as the Chinese had been though. They didn't talk much. The waiters didn't either, they just came and went, sliding plates on to the table. Even the dish that was sizzling didn't raise much joy. The wallpaper was dark red, so was the carpet; the lighting was very low, so, because of the Mood, it was like being inside a big, dull mouth after a while.

There was a picture of Lake Windermere on the wall, which irritated Laura very much because she said it should be a picture of somewhere in India, not England.

'Why?' asked Vixen. 'We are in England.'

'But it's an Indian restaurant.'

'So?' asked Vixen stubbornly. 'Maybe they want to . . . ' She paused, chapatti held in the air, trying to remember a rather good phrase she had heard Greg use once . . . She remembered it: 'Maybe they want to embrace both cultures.'

Laura just looked at her oddly. Vixen couldn't guess what she was thinking.

The dish immediately between them was the one that had been sizzling when it first came in. It definitely wasn't now.

Vixen thought they were both probably quite glad to part company that evening. Her mother went off with that desperate haunted quality about her—stronger than ever. Vixen felt extremely mixed up and fretful.

48

When she got back, she found that her father had come home and been puzzled to find hair-grips all over the place, like the spilling of an actress's casket. Then he saw what remained of Vixen's hairstyle and understood.

'It doesn't know whether it's up or down,' he remarked cheerfully.

'No,' said Vixen. 'It doesn't.'

He had the hair-grips gathered in his hand.

'Just out of interest,' she asked. 'How many did I spill?'

'What do you want to know that for?' he asked—but he did count them.

'Thirteen,' he said.

SEVEN

The next evening, Nana and Grandad came round because they had 'sorted out' a holiday for Vixen.

She wasn't at all sure how she felt about this: there didn't seem to be any choice offered her—and she hadn't before been away without her father or a friend.

She was sitting cross-legged on the living room floor, alternating between reading a novel and writing one. She wondered if her dad was tempted to suggest 'plagiarizing' again but he didn't say anything. He was watching television, his legs stretched out in front of him, displaying a hole in his sock.

'That's not like you,' said Vixen, 'and Nana's bound to remark on it.'

'That's right,' said Kevin and got up to change it. But before he had reached the door, the front door knocker rattled.

'Oh well,' he said and went to open it.

'The Cotswolds,' said Nana impressively.

'And very nice too,' added Grandad because Vixen didn't.

'The Cotswolds,' said Nana again.

Vixen still said nothing.

'Er . . . which part?' asked Kevin.

Vixen glanced at him, assuming he was thinking the same as she was . . .

'A village near Worcester,' continued Nana. 'Well—'

'My mum comes from a village near Worcester,' interrupted Vixen. 'Remember?'

There was a dead, blank silence. Nana still had her mouth open. Kevin took a long swig of wine.

'It must have been that that made you think of it,' said Vixen. 'You know . . . subconsciously. Because you've never been there, have you?'

'None of us have,' said Kevin faintly.

'But . . . but,' spluttered Nana. 'There must be hundreds of villages near Worcester. It's not very likely to be the same one, now is it?'

'And so what if it is anyway?' said Vixen sullenly.

Everyone twiddled with shoelaces or buttons for a couple of seconds.

Nana took a deep breath:

'Well anyway . . . ' she said. 'We rang Dorothy because she's always going to the Cotswold villages and she put me on to another nice lady called Nancy . . . '

'Who's Nancy?' asked Vixen.

'A friend of Dorothy's.'

'Who's Dorothy?'

'Oh, Vixen, don't be exasperating! You know perfectly well who Dorothy is!'

Vixen grudgingly admitted that she knew her to be Nana's best friend.

'And Nancy is a friend of hers,' continued Nana, 'who runs a boarding house just outside the village near Worcester—and she says she's quite happy to have you for a week.'

'On my own?' asked Vixen, aghast.

Kevin looked terribly guilty but Nana said:

'No! That's the best thing about it! Nancy has a little boy who's very close in age to Vixen.'

'Which way "very close"?' asked Vixen. 'Up or down?'

'He's less than two years younger and Nancy said he could do with the company.'

'But I don't play with little boys younger than me!' protested Vixen.

'He's a very nice little boy,' said Nana stoutly.

'How do you know? Have you met him?'

'Well, no, but . . . '

'Vixen,' said her father gently. 'You don't have to go if you don't want to.'

'Well, there's gratitude for you, I must say!' exclaimed Nana. 'We go and arrange a nice holiday for Vixen and—'

Vixen interrupted:

'Are there lots of fields and woods I can go running in?' she asked.

'Oh yes!' chorused all three adults together.

'And is the boarding house really old and big and interesting?'

'Oh yes,' said Nana.

'Has it got a big garden?'

'Oh yes.'

'And will I have to be with the boy all the time or will I be able to write my book? And read other people's?'

'Of course you'll be able to write if you want to,' said Kevin firmly before Nana could speak. 'And I'll try to come and join you for a day or two.'

'In that case,' said Vixen politely, 'thank you very much for "arranging my holiday", Nana.'

They opened another bottle of wine and Nana and Grandad stayed until it was drunk. Kevin saw them to the door then, leaving Vixen staring ahead of her, thinking. Her books and pens were cast aside for the moment. The Cotswolds, she thought. Rhona is going to Jamaica this summer and Georgette is going to Spain and I'm going to the Cotswolds.

From the front door, she could faintly hear the end of Nana's goodbye sentence:

' . . . in your sock, Kevin . . . '

EIGHT

The following week, on his day off, Kevin drove Vixen to the Cotswolds.

'Would this be real fox-country?' asked Vixen.

'Yes, yes, it would,' said Kevin, hoping to encourage her.

They saw one as well—an old dog-fox with a greying snout stretched out asleep in a pool of sunlight. He looked so peaceful that Vixen got anxious for him. After all, in her fox-state, he could have been her grandfather.

'Unusual to see one in the daytime,' commented Kevin.

'They don't hunt foxes around here, do they?' she asked suspiciously.

'Well . . . ' said her human-state father.

She shuddered.

They were passing through almost impossibly neat little villages with more signs for 'Afternoon Tea' than Vixen had seen in her life. Even the ducks on the ponds were very bright and plastic-looking.

'I bet they never get stale bread,' said Vixen.

'More like jam tarts and custard slices,' said Kevin.

You couldn't imagine anyone getting drunk in the pubs or causing a diversion on the village greens.

'Don't be deceived, Vixen,' said Kevin, loading fuel on to her imagination. 'It may look all neat and manicured but there's menace and malice behind some of those net curtains . . . '

Vixen stared at him.

'And feuds,' he continued. 'And probably madness.'

'In the lanes they smile and say hello . . . ' murmured Vixen, taking up the theme, 'but Dark Intent is always lurking.'

'The woods over there look sinister, don't they?' said Kevin, pointing at a murky, blue-ish clutch of trees in the distance. 'That's probably where they all go to become their real selves.'

They drove into yet another small village and a middle-aged woman was walking down the main street, wearing a big, bossy kilt even though it was summer, and a red cotton jumper.

'She must be boiling!' said Vixen.

'Well, her feet are in sandals anyway,' said Kevin, slyly echoing his mother.

The woman had intent in her face—the intent that goes, even these days, with Women's Institutes, Church fêtes, and doing useful 'crafts' at home with egg boxes.

'But I bet the pink roses up her walls have got more thorns than anyone else's,' said Vixen.

But the next village, where they stopped to consult the map, had someone quite different in it.

An elderly woman was walking here. She had a handsome but ravaged face which immediately caught the attention of both Vixen and her father. For some reason, they both shivered.

'She's not hiding anything, is she?' said Vixen. 'I bet she looks like what she is.'

The woman was very tall, and was wearing what looked like a floating grey chiffon dress. In fact, it could have been an expensive dressing gown but they decided it probably wasn't. Her shoes were grey, too, with cuban heels and bar-straps. She had pearls at her neck, powder on her face and mulberry-coloured lipstick on her mouth. There was something not quite 'right' about her—whatever 'right' is—and not just because she was wearing odd clothes for the time of day.

'I don't know why,' said Vixen, 'but she reminds me of Mum.'

'Funny you should say that,' said Kevin awkwardly. 'I was thinking the same thing.'

'It's the height,' said Vixen, 'and she looks hunted like Mum does.'

Kevin didn't answer.

'Not the clothes of course,' continued Vixen.

'No, no, not the clothes.'

'And Mum of course is much younger . . . '

Completely unexpectedly, the woman went into a pub.

'Well, well,' said Kevin. 'I would have thought she was too elevated for that.'

This village was the one they needed to be in. The 'House' where Vixen was to stay was just outside it.

'Isn't it funny it hasn't got a name?' said Kevin. 'It's just called "The House".'

The House had a long, gravelly driveway with high hedges at the start of it. There was a wooden board on a pole leaning out over the road. On an inky blue background, in silver letters, like stars in the night sky, it read:

THE HOUSE
Boarding House

And that was all.

'Repetition of the word, "house",' said Kevin. 'You'd get shouted at for that in English lessons, wouldn't you?'

'It sounds better than "Bed And Breakfast" though,' said Vixen. 'That's really basic and unimaginative.'

'The House' itself was very far from basic and unimaginative. It was rather stunning. Vixen and Kevin both gasped as the car turned the bend in the drive and an old, sandstone building with all sorts of curious, intricate windows loomed up in front of them.

'Oh,' said Vixen, her eyes shining.

'This will inspire you,' said Kevin.

He stopped the car and they gladly got out.

Their shoes scrunched on the gravel and they made their way to the front door. Before they got there, it was opened.

A woman was standing there, smiling. She looked to be in her mid forties with an anxious, but friendly, face.

'Mr Courtney?' she said. 'And . . . ' She paused for a moment as if she had difficulty with the next name. 'And . . . Vixen?'

'Yes,' they replied together.

Everyone smiled and shook hands.

'You're later than I thought you'd be,' she said. 'So Douglas isn't here at the moment, I'm afraid.'

'Douglas?'

'My son,' she said—and something about the way she said it made Vixen stare at her. It was as if a glow lit her up from within.

'He's gone on an errand,' said the woman (Nancy).

'An errand!' said Vixen. 'That's an old fashioned thing to do!'

Nancy laughed.

'Oh yes,' she said. 'He's a good boy. He's always doing things for me.'

Vixen just stared. She wasn't used to children over the age of five being referred to as 'good boys' and 'good girls'. For goodness sake, she thought, he's nearly a teenager. Then Nancy said something else about him and she thought: she adores him. She just adores him. What's that going to be like to stay with? She knew her own father adored her—though he didn't show it as obviously (for which she was glad). And her mother . . . who knew?

Nancy drew them into a large-ish entrance hall with a big fireplace. It was very cool in there—almost cold, although it was the middle of the summer. If the fire had been lit, it might not have been too much. She took them into a little room to the side of the front door and they sighed with relief because it was warm again. The sun streamed in through the window and allotted itself to one particular chair.

'Do sit down,' said Nancy.

Vixen hesitated for a moment for 'manners' but saw no one else was going to take that chair so sank into it herself. It was like being in a spotlight.

Kevin stayed for about an hour while Nancy served them with tea and three different kinds of scone: some with raisins, some without raisins, and some with cheese—all home-made. Vixen could tell her dad was rather impressed. Douglas continued to be away on his 'errand' but he was still there in the room in spirit because Nancy talked about him more than Vixen had heard any other parent talk about a child ever. She didn't mention a partner of any sort, so Vixen assumed she was on her own and her son was everything to her. She had an idle fancy for a moment wondering if her dad would find Nancy attractive—but then he said he had to get home because he and Greg were doing something that night.

'I'll miss you, Vixen,' he said quite sadly.

'Well stay then!' said Vixen impetuously. 'Maybe Nancy's got room for you too!'

'Yes, I have,' said Nancy at once. 'I'm not up to full capacity with boarders at the moment.'

'No, no, I've got to work,' said Kevin at once.

Vixen wondered if the time would ever come when holidays didn't terrify him.

After he'd gone, Nancy showed her round the house—into every room except the boarders' bedrooms.

'I don't take many at once,' she said. 'There's only three lots at the moment. A couple, and a retired gentleman, and a lady who I think is here to sketch or something.'

Vixen thought the last one sounded the most interesting.

'This is the boarders' sitting room,' said Nancy, throwing open the door of a huge upstairs room.

'And this is the sitting room for me and Dougie,' she said, opening a smaller room on the ground floor.

The first thing Vixen saw in here was a wooden string puppet lying in the middle of the floor, as if it had been abandoned in a hurry.

'Well, how strange,' said Nancy. 'That's not like Douglas. He's usually so careful with his things.'

Vixen resisted the impulse to say 'Well, of course, he's perfect, isn't he' and went to pick the puppet up instead.

'It's a fox!' she said. 'And I think I've seen one like it before—except that that one was white!'

She held it up by its wooden controls.

'Where shall I put it?' she asked Nancy.

'Oh, anywhere for now, dear.'

Vixen put it on a blue velvet armchair.

'Do I have to stick to the boarders' sitting room?' she asked rather fearfully, trying to imagine how she'd get on with 'the couple' and the 'retired gentleman'. 'The lady who wanted to sketch' would probably be less of an ordeal.

'No of course not! I'm not thinking of you as one of the boarders. You're our house guest. You can share this room with me and Dougie.'

Am I ever to meet this 'Dougie', Vixen wondered. He's a long time on his errand . . .

'Thank you very much,' she said to Nancy.

A little while later, she was wandering in the gardens at will, intoxicated with sun. Nancy had told her that some of the areas were marked 'PRIVATE' but that only applied to the 'boarders' not to her. This made her feel privileged. She made a point of going to those parts first:

there was a vegetable garden and a high hedge at the bottom of it with a door in it. Vixen was making her way, past the onions, for the door when she heard Nancy's voice, as if in a sun-drenched dream, behind her:

'Victoria, dear! Here's Douglas!'

She turned round slowly and dreamily and saw Nancy with a boy standing next to her. He was surrounded by shopping bags which had presumably been his 'errand'. She was startled to see that he was dressed entirely in white and it was so bright, it dazzled her. These must be his errand clothes, she thought—and she staggered slightly. There was something piercingly familiar about his face but she couldn't place it. Eeriest of all, by some trick of the sunlight, she could almost have sworn he was wearing a halo. It was too much for Vixen: she did something she had never done before. There was a rushing in her ears, the ground seemed to leap up to meet her, and she fainted. Right across the onion bed too.

NINE

She recovered consciousness just a few seconds later—
onion stalks brushing her hair and earth crumbling
round her like fruit cake.

Nancy was bending over her anxiously.

'Oh, I'm so sorry,' murmured Vixen dizzily. 'How
embarrassing.'

'Do you do this often, dear?' asked Nancy.

'Oh no, no, not at all!' said Vixen, struggling to sit up
and horrified that Nancy might think she was fragile.
Douglas was there, handing her a glass of water.

She took it, trembling, as if the giver was an unearthly
presence. But:

'There's earth all over you,' said Douglas in a
perfectly normal voice.

Vixen suddenly noticed that her glass of water had ice
in it—and a slice of lemon and a slice of lime. She was
quite touched by this attention, but embarrassed about
being waited on.

'Good job it wasn't you falling in the onion bed,' she
said to Douglas. 'All dressed in white like that.'

'I'll change later,' said Douglas simply.

Vixen decided it really was time she got out of their
onion bed. She stood up on shaky legs, the lemon and
lime swimming about in her drink like little boats. She
stepped on to the path and drank the water.

'Thank you,' she said.

'Would you like to see my garden?' asked Douglas
unexpectedly.

'Yes, go and look at Dougie's garden,' said Nancy
with relief. 'I must prepare dinner for tonight.'

Dougie's garden was the one through the door in

the hedge at the bottom of the vegetables. He led the way.

He pushed the door open and stood back politely for Vixen to go through first. It seemed an oddly old-fashioned gesture for a boy who was only eleven.

'Thank you,' said Vixen. She knew that Nana and Auntie Margaret would describe him as 'very well brought up'. Normally, this would put her off people—but there was something likeable about Douglas.

'This is my garden,' he said.

Vixen nearly fainted again with astonishment and admiration.

'You mean you've done all this yourself?' she asked.

'My mum helped me at the beginning,' he said.

The garden was quite small, with the high hedge all the way round the flower beds and little twisting paths between them all. There were lupins and roses and sweet peas and heathers and what seemed to be hundreds of others all raising their heads and spreading their leaves in a dreaming medley of colour and fragrance. Vixen just stood and stared at it. Then she saw Douglas suddenly frown and pull at a weed (probably the only one in the whole place). He got it up with a deft, efficient movement which vividly reminded her of someone else but she couldn't think who. She thought it was an adult rather than another child—which was odd.

They walked past the boarders' dining room on their way to their own dinner.

The door was ajar.

Vixen peered in because she was curious to see the boarders—particularly the 'lady sketch artist'. It was a long, narrow room with a highly polished wooden floor which made her think of skating rather than eating. The evening sun was streaming in and a girl who looked about sixteen was walking very carefully through it, carrying dishes of soup. She was wearing a short, black skirt, a black shirt, and flat, black leather shoes. She picked her way over the treacherous-looking floor.

'She's the waitress,' said Douglas matter-of-factly. 'She lives in the village.'

'There's no steam coming off that soup,' said Vixen.

'That's because it's chilled,' said Douglas.

'Cold soup?'

'Yes. For the summer. Tonight, it's chilled avocado with hand-chopped chives. Turned in a blender with . . . '

Something about the way he was doing this again reminded Vixen of somebody else. She still couldn't think who it was though.

There were only two boarders in the room and they were sitting at different tables, both with their heads down over papers. Vixen assumed that these two were the 'retired gentleman' and the 'lady sketch artist' to use Nancy's language. She couldn't imagine Nancy saying 'man' and 'woman'. There was no sign of 'the couple'. The 'lady sketch artist' looked about forty and she had lots of wheat-coloured hair with grey streaks all piled in various bumps and hillocks on her head.

'Come on,' said Douglas. 'We'll be late for our own soup.'

'It'll be getting cold, ha, ha,' said Vixen.

He smiled.

TEN

Not surprisingly, Vixen couldn't sleep that night. The room she was in was very large, and the bed was the biggest she had seen in her life. There was a prodigious chest of drawers pushed back against one wall, and a wardrobe like something in a museum looming against another. Separating them all was a sea of green carpet. Vixen's black plimsolls were curious little islands in the middle of it—one lying on its side, the other, standing up.

Douglas's face seemed to be floating in front of her all night . . . at one point, she nearly got up and rang her father just for the sound of a voice she was familiar with. But then, Douglas seemed familiar too . . .

She tossed and turned in the darkness and the heat—gave up on that and paced the room. Her bare feet marked out a passage in the green carpet. She was just about to turn on the lamp and see what the time was when she suddenly heard singing from underneath her . . .

Someone's just turned the television on, she thought. But when she lit the lamp and saw it was three in the morning, she thought maybe it wasn't that. The radio then? Somebody lying in bed in the dark and listening? Again, she didn't think it was very likely. She lay down on the floor, put her ear against it and listened intently. Now, she realized it was children singing. They had high, reedy voices slightly out of tune and they were singing the same thing over and over again. Then, suddenly, they stopped. Vixen sat upright. She didn't particularly know it but she looked just like a little fox at that moment—the pointed face intense with listening.

The sounds came back—but they weren't singing this time, they were murmuring. Then, unexpectedly, the wailing cry of a baby rose up. Immediately, like a switch being flicked, the singing started again—the same tune as before.

They're trying to soothe the baby, thought Vixen. The baby's upset and they want to distract it so they're singing . . .

But who are they all for goodness sake?

She didn't recognize the song but it sounded like an old nursery rhyme and it was haunting and eerie like a lot of them can be—even more so in the dead of the night.

She tried to make out the words.

It was something like:

'Wind the bobbin up,

Wind the bobbin up . . . ' then something else to do with sewing (a lot of nursery rhymes had references to sewing, she realized), then something about a candle and the dusk and . . .

'Drain the goblet to the dregs . . . '

Then it stopped again.

She waited for several minutes but it didn't start a third time.

It was nearly light now. The time was quarter to five. Vixen got up from the floor and went to the window with that wild, strained feeling round the eyes that happens when you haven't slept the night. She felt shaky too. She drew back the curtains, opened the window and leaned out. Then she nearly cried out with delight at what she saw—but stopped herself in time because that would have frightened the creatures.

Young foxes were playing on the lawn. They were cuffing each other and tumbling about—all in a whirl of noses, ears, and bushy tails . . . As she looked more though, she realized there was something odd about them . . . they seemed curiously insubstantial even though she was seeing them in almost full daylight. Then it dawned on her what it was! It was like watching a black and white film when you had expected colour: they weren't red . . . they were grey. And not just grey, but shadowy. She rubbed her eyes and leaned further out of the window. Was it her imagination or were they actually fading? In another couple of moments they had gone altogether—and not, she could have sworn, because they had run off: it was because they had simply disappeared . . .

Nancy asked her if she had slept well—and she found herself going automatically into 'yes thank you' and realized how many other times she had said that to be polite and hadn't meant it. Douglas was staring at her though.

'But you've got big shadows round your eyes,' he said.

'That's because I couldn't sleep,' said Vixen.

'Oh dear,' said Nancy at once and stared at her in concern.

For a fleeting moment, Vixen couldn't help wondering if this concern was really for her, or whether it was for the reflection it would have on Nancy as 'carer' in the eyes of her father . . . After all, Nancy didn't really seem to care about anyone in the world except Douglas.

But she relented. After all, Nancy was nice.

'I saw foxes in the early morning,' said Vixen. 'Young ones. Loads of them. Playing on the lawn. But—'

She stopped because both Nancy and Douglas were looking at her oddly.

'You saw the foxes?' said Nancy—and, for some reason, the 'the' made it sound rather sinister.

'But she would though, wouldn't she, Mum?' said Douglas after a pause. 'She's got an affinity with foxes.'

Vixen thought 'affinity' was a big word for an eleven

year old but that was typical of Douglas. Nancy's face was pinched and stiff.

'I've lived here all my life,' she said. 'But I've never seen the foxes.'

'But have you looked?' asked Douglas reasonably.

'Of course I've looked!' she snapped—and Vixen was amazed to hear her speak to Douglas so sharply. Up until then, it had been nothing but deepest pride and devotion.

He was struck by it too: he was staring at his mother with his butter knife raised, flat and immobile, over his slice of granary bread.

She began to make it up to him immediately.

'Open the lime marmalade, Dougie,' she said, sounding tragic. 'You know you prefer it to the orange.'

'No, it's all right,' he said and put his knife back into action. Vixen watched it slide with a gleam into the jar of streaky orange substance. She had never liked marmalade—but her dad did. And he made his own. It wouldn't have surprised her to learn that Dougie did too. She and Nancy watched, mesmerized, while Dougie spread the marmalade neatly on his bread. Their hypnotic staring didn't trouble him: he just calmly lifted the orange and brown slice to his mouth.

Vixen mentally shook herself.

'Is there something special about the foxes?' she asked.

'Not many people have ever seen them,' said Douglas. 'They—'

'More tea, Vixen, dear?' asked Nancy just a little too brightly.

'What does it mean if you do see them?' persisted Vixen.

'In your case, it's probably just because you're called Vixen,' said Nancy, but she sounded as if she was starting to panic.

'Oh no, Mum,' said Douglas. 'There's more to it than that. Isn't the story that if—'

'Just a silly myth, just a silly myth!' Nancy almost screamed.

Douglas stared at her again.

'What's the matter, Mum?' he asked.

She didn't answer, but took a long swig of tea and the hand that held the cup was trembling.

Vixen decided she may as well be hung for a sheep as a lamb—or for a vixen as a cub. The foxes she had seen seemed to cause Nancy some distress but she had to mention the singing too otherwise the picture of her night would not be complete.

'You said there was a couple staying here,' she said.

'Yes that's right,' said Nancy, relieved. Flesh and blood guests in her boarding house were things she felt happy about discussing.

'Have they got any children?'

Nancy looked puzzled.

'No, dear. Why?'

Vixen launched herself into it:

'Because last night I heard children singing. I think it was an old nursery rhyme or a hymn or something and they were obviously trying to shut a baby up . . . I mean, soothe it and . . . '

Vixen didn't happen to be looking at Nancy while she said all this. She was skewering some crumbs on her plate with her knife. So she didn't see the expression on Nancy's face. But Douglas was suddenly terribly interested.

'There's another story connected with the house!' he said.

'Is there?' said Nancy sharply. 'I never heard any other.'

But Douglas carried on.

'Yes there is, Mum,' he said. 'Apparently, in the last

century, a woman in the village sold a baby to someone in this house and—' He stopped because he had to. Nancy had risen to her feet and her face was white with anger. Vixen was frankly staring—and even the cool Douglas recoiled.

'From whom did you hear that story?' she demanded.

'S-someone in the village,' said Douglas.

'It's all rubbish!' she cried. 'Just a silly story! Vixen must have . . . must have imagined the singing—or she must have been dreaming.'

'I wasn't dreaming,' said Vixen stubbornly. 'How could I? I wasn't asleep.'

ELEVEN

Nancy was at work in the laundry room which was a spacious, tiled room in the basement. It was hot and steamy like a Victorian washer-room scene in a film—and Vixen and Douglas left her to go for a walk. Nancy was still tight-lipped and upset and they still didn't really know why. She was pulling damp sheets out of the washing machines—they were made all twisted and thin by the water and looked like shrouds.

'Let's go to the woods,' said Dougie in his precise way.

They set off along the lane and through a field.

'My friend will probably be in the woods,' added Douglas.

Vixen wondered what he'd be like.

They didn't say very much for the first few feet of the field—Nancy's distressed countenance was probably still floating in their heads.

All the same though, Vixen had to know what the answer to something was.

'You can tell me now,' she said. 'What does it mean if you see the foxes?'

Dougie hesitated for a moment—presumably because he thought his mother would be angry if he told her.

He did tell though.

'The story is,' he said, 'that if someone sees the foxes—those particular ones, I mean, not just any old foxes—then it means that they're going to uncover a big secret.'

'A secret?'

'To do with the house.'

Vixen felt shivers going up and down her spine.

'Is that why your mum wants to see them?' she asked. 'Because she wants to find out a secret?'

'I don't know,' said Douglas uncomfortably.

They walked in silence for a few minutes. Coarse stalks of grass lashed their shins. The field was going uphill towards the woods. Stepping under the trees from the hot field meant an instant change of temperature. Almost enough to make you shiver.

'That's better, isn't it?' said Douglas.

There was a stillness in there—but somehow, it wasn't peaceful. It was as if the trees were holding their breath, waiting for something to happen. Vixen felt uneasy, but Douglas seemed totally unconcerned.

'Let's see if my friend's in the loggy glade,' he said, and a dry twig snapped under his foot.

'Boggy glade?'

'No, not boggy. I've never seen it boggy. I said loggy. There's logs in it. My friend sits on them.'

That's a very static pastime for a young boy, thought Vixen, but she didn't say anything.

When they came to the glade, it meant being drenched in sunlight again. Sure enough there were logs there, surrounded by thirsty grass.

'Here's my friend,' said Dougie proudly.

And Vixen stared in astonishment: it wasn't another eleven-year-old boy; it was an elderly woman. And she knew she had seen her before though it took her a moment to remember where: it was the woman she and her father had seen in the village on their way to The House—the one who had oddly reminded Vixen of her mother.

Today, this lady was wearing a flowered, silk dress, very carefully tailored and belted; a string of pearls, cream shoes, and a large, floppy, straw hat (it wasn't the clothes that reminded Vixen of Laura—it was the air she had). She looked as if she should be at a

70

Buckingham Palace garden party, not sitting absurdly on a log in a Cotswold wood.

And yet, it wasn't absurd. Not when she raised her ravaged face from under the wide hat-brim and looked at them. Disturbing, not absurd. To Vixen anyway.

The woman smiled at Douglas and Vixen was further alarmed by the possessiveness in her eyes.

'It's the boy,' said the woman. Her voice was exactly as Vixen would have imagined—upper-crust and strident—and cracked with age.

Douglas was fussing around her: the woman was sitting on a tartan rug and he was spreading the sides out further for her. He even arranged the fringes so all the strands were stretched out straight like fingers.

'Someone else,' she said sharply. 'There's someone else here. A girl.'

'Yes, she's come with me,' said Douglas. 'She's called Vixen.'

The woman stiffened. She stared at Vixen through narrowed eyes.

'I've heard that before,' she said. 'Can't think where . . . '

Vixen stared back but her heart was thumping hard. There was something menacing and predatory about this woman in the flowered dress on the log.

'It's short for Victoria,' she heard herself say.

The woman was looking her up and down.

'You look like a fox,' she said.

Vixen was very tempted to say 'Well, I've never heard that before', but didn't think sarcasm would work on this person.

'Something else,' the woman was muttering. 'Heard it before . . . ' Then she looked straight into the trees beyond them and said: 'Is William there?' But now she sounded as if she were about to cry.

71

Vixen turned round sharply but there was no one in the trees.

'No, not William,' said Dougie cheerfully. 'Just me—Douglas. And Vixen.'

'Who's William?' Vixen hissed at him.

Douglas shrugged his shoulders. 'I don't know.'

The woman's face was still folded up as if tears were coming. Then suddenly she smoothed it out. 'Sit down,' she said to Douglas with the possessive gleam back in her eye. 'Sit down and we'll chat.'

Dougie indicated that Vixen was to sit down too. She did reluctantly, wondering why Dougie didn't seem to find anything odd about the woman. Or maybe he did, but it didn't bother him. The woman (no name had yet been attributed to her) then proceeded to hold court.

It was mostly along the lines of 'the way things used to be' and Vixen, observing Douglas as discreetly as she could, could see that he was completely engrossed and drawn by the teller. It was almost worrying. Every so often, the woman would stop in her tale, look slightly confused, mutter something—then start again.

Vixen's gaze wandered behind the log at one point and, partly hidden by foliage, she thought she could discern the long, green neck of a bottle. Of course, this could have been left there by somebody else—it didn't necessarily mean that the woman had brought it.

Vixen smiled to herself at the idea of this woman in her floating dress and pearls swigging from the bottle like a pirate—but then she saw a glass with a stem, pertly sticking up beside the bottle. Big green leaves were brushing against them.

There was another pause in the narration: this time, the woman was staring ahead for quite a long time.

'Shall we go for a walk now, Dougie?' suggested Vixen. 'Maybe—'

The woman then snapped at her so abruptly that she jumped.

'Foxy, foxy . . . ' she was saying. 'Vixens should run, not walk. Run . . . or they'll be caught . . . ' She said it as if she were on the side of the riders and hounds, not the foxes.

'I like running,' said Vixen with dignity—but she was starting to shake. Douglas, on the other hand, stretched himself as if he were waking from a delightful dream.

'We'll go now,' he said politely, 'and let you rest.' He stood up and brushed the leaves and twigs from his knees—again with an oddly adult gesture.

He's too old for his years, thought Vixen. But there again . . . was he still childish enough to be taken in by a strange old woman?

'Goodbye,' said Douglas. 'We'll see you again soon.'

'Goodbye, boy,' said the woman and then took to staring ahead again.

'Goodbye,' said Vixen, determined to be acknowledged.

'Goodbye . . . ' said the woman and it came out in a cracked whisper.

Well, at least the menace has gone, thought Vixen, but, while she was still looking, the woman turned her head and gave her a heavy-lidded, baleful glare. Vixen glared back—but only briefly. Being Polite To Older People had not been drummed into her for nothing. As soon as she judged they were out of earshot, she challenged Douglas.

'Well, who's that?' she asked.

'My friend,' said Douglas.

Was she imagining it or did Vixen detect a touch of defensiveness on his part?

'Don't you think there's something very strange about her?' she continued.

'So? I like her.'

'Haven't you got friends of your own age?' asked Vixen curiously.

'Yes,' he said, but she wasn't sure if she believed him.

Dougie stopped in the field and started gathering cornflowers.

'My mum likes these,' he said.

Vixen had a sudden startling vision of two people with nets in Dougie's life: one was his mother who cast him about with devotion and the other was the woman in the wood who drew him in with her stories and looked at him with hungry, possessive eyes. For the first time, she actually saw Douglas as rather vulnerable. Before that, he had just seemed an efficient, self-possessed young boy.

'Do you even know her name?' she persisted.

'Whose name?'

'The woman's in the wood, of course!'

' 'Course I do. It's Alice.'

'Alice what?'

'Don't know. Does it matter?'

Vixen stared at him. He was standing in the long grass of the field, holding the stems of three cornflowers. His hand was grasping them really hard and the flowers stuck straight up in the air like rods. There was an obstinate set to his lips which she had never seen before.

'You're really drawn by her, aren't you?' said Vixen. 'By the wom— by Alice, I mean.'

Douglas just stood there with his flowers, like a statue.

'Does your mum know about her?' Oh God, I sound just like Nana and Auntie Margaret, thought Vixen. Except that in their case, it would be 'Does your dad know?' Definitely not her mother!

Douglas moved at last.

'No, she doesn't,' he said.

'Why not?'

'Because . . . because she doesn't need to know . . . '

He looked at her fearfully.

'Well don't worry, I'm not going to tell her,' said Vixen at once.

She did tell her own father though. When she rang him that night, she told him how odd she found it that an eleven-year-old boy wanted to be friends with an old woman who wasn't a relation.

'Well, there's no harm in it, is there?' said Kevin cautiously.

'Well, I think she might be an alcoholic,' said Vixen. 'And she's very possessive.'

'Ah . . . ' said Kevin.

'And she's so strange.'

'Well, if you get really concerned about it, tell his mother.'

Vixen realized that this was of course an option—but it really was an unwritten rule amongst friends that you didn't tell their parents things that they wouldn't tell them themselves.

And then she woke up to the fact that she hadn't told Kevin about the voices she had heard last night or the eerie foxes she had seen in the early morning. Now why was that? It was simply because something inexplicable stopped her. And presumably something stopped Douglas from telling his mother about his friend in the wood . . .

TWELVE

She heard the voices again. This time, she was asleep when they started and they woke her up. She lay there for a few minutes letting the various sensations wash over her: curiosity and bewilderment and fear. Then she sat up.

It was the same song at first, sung in the same young reedy voices:

'Wind the bobbin up, wind the bobbin up . . . '

She listened to it from beginning to end. Then there was a pause and the wail of the baby rose up like last time. She expected them to start the same song again but they didn't . . . they obviously decided to give up on singing the baby to sleep and thought they'd entertain it instead: this second song was much faster and livelier:

'Without a warner
She ran round the corner . . . '

And then:

'Tally-ho! Tally-ho!
Which way did the vixen go?'

When she heard that, Vixen's whole body stiffened—but only for an instant. Then she was off—out of the bed, out of the room, and running down the corridor to Douglas's room.

She knocked on Douglas's door, trying not to be too loud because she didn't want to wake Nancy as well.

'Who's there?' he said eventually, his voice croaky with sleep.

'It's me!' said Vixen in an agitated whisper. 'Can I come in please?'

There was a pause.

'Hang on a minute,' he said.

She guessed he was one of those people who don't like being seen all dishevelled and vulnerable.

All this time, the singing was still going on. There was a creak as Douglas got out of his bed. Then she heard him padding about, probably getting into slippers and dressing gown. She was ready to scream with impatience before he finally opened the door.

'Listen!' she said at once. 'They're singing again!'

'What?' said Douglas.

'The children are singing! You can hear them underneath us!'

'I can't hear anything,' said Douglas.

'Open the door wider!'

He did.

'There!' she said.

He cocked his head like a dog.

'No,' he said. 'I still can't hear anything.'

'Oh, Douglas, you must be able to!' she cried.

He frowned with concentration. Then:

'No,' he said. 'I definitely can't.'

She grabbed his hand and pulled him out of the room.

'Let's go downstairs,' she said, 'and find out where it's coming from.'

He didn't argue, but looked at her as if he were twice her age, which annoyed her.

They started to float down the stairs, a barefoot vixen and a carefully-slippered Douglas.

The singing, she realized, wasn't getting any louder the nearer they got to it, which was very odd. Rather frantically, she opened all the doors of the downstairs rooms, one after the other, but all of them were empty. And then the singing suddenly stopped.

'Douglas,' she said in an alarmed semi-whisper, 'tell me again that story connected to the house.'

'Which one?'

'The one about the baby.'

They were standing in the hall, where it was colder than anywhere else in the house—cold enough for a fire not to be too much even in the summer. Douglas pulled his dressing gown cord tighter.

'The story is,' he said, 'that someone in the last century lived in the village and she had a baby but she didn't mean to and she didn't have any money and she panicked and there was someone living in this house who wanted another one and she couldn't have another one and she did have money so she bought it off her and they both tried to keep it a secret . . . '

He said it all quickly and breathlessly, which was not his usual style of speech. He was looking around as well as if he were frightened his mother would hear him and be angry.

'They'd be very anxious to keep the baby soothed and quiet, wouldn't they?' said Vixen. 'They'd try singing to it for hours and everything. They'd probably do more for that one than for one of their own because it was stolen.'

'Not stolen,' said Douglas promptly. 'Bought.'

'Bought then. Sold. Bought.'

They both just stood there for a couple of seconds. Vixen shivered in a way that you shouldn't in the summer.

'Would you like a cup of tea?' asked Douglas suddenly.

Vixen laughed. Young though they both were, they were relentlessly English about tea. She and Douglas went into the kitchen which was much warmer than the hall. He went about things in his usual deft, efficient, curiously adult way. He even offered her a choice of tea: Earl Grey or Breakfast Blend.

'Breakfast Blend, please,' she said—and then, affectionately, 'you sounded just like my dad then.'

That was it! It was her father that Douglas reminded her of! Why had it taken her so long to realize?

Probably because it wasn't usual for a child to remind you of an adult unless they were related.

She stared at him as he handed her a steaming mug with wild animals on it. She didn't look closely but she assumed they were foxes. He didn't seem to notice her staring but sat down across the table from her with his own tea. His mug had teddy bears in suits and ties on it which, Vixen reflected, was a good representation of what he was himself.

It was a companionable few minutes in the deep of the night, with the tiles of the kitchen marching all round them showing off their comfortable vegetable motifs and the tea like hot nectar in the highly-patterned mugs.

Vixen didn't think there would be any more singing tonight.

THIRTEEN

Next day, Nancy awkwardly announced that she was taking them out to lunch 'for a treat'. She was obviously feeling guilty because she had been grumpy and snappish the day before and wanted to make it up to them.

'Where?' asked Dougie in surprise.

This was obviously not something they did often.

'Oh, I don't know,' said Nancy, flustered. 'There's a restaurant in the village, isn't there?'

'Only pubs,' said Douglas. 'The King's Arms, The Three Travellers, and The Old Red Fox.'

'Well, one of them will be all right, won't it? There'll be a family room we can eat in?'

Vixen cringed at the expression 'family room'. It immediately conjured up images of big bouncy coloured things between the tables with big, bouncy toddlers sabotaging them. 'Family rooms' were not something she had ever been taken to as a child because most of the time her family only consisted of two.

The Old Red Fox was where they ended up of course . . . Some people might have found the everlasting attention to their nickname exhausting but Vixen never minded.

They chose a table in a corner and sat there awkwardly for a few minutes.

'Er . . . do we ask for menus or do you think they bring them to us?' said Nancy.

She was surprisingly ill at ease considering she ran an establishment of her own.

'You probably go to the bar and order it yourself,' said Vixen. 'I'll go and look and then come back and tell you what there is.'

She was quite glad to get up and move away for a few minutes—Nancy was making her tense. She went up to the bar where there was a blackboard with three chalk messages on it:

ROAST BEEF
ROAST LAMB
ROAST CHICKEN

Well, that was easy enough—if somewhat unoriginal. Vixen went back over to the other side of the room to relay this. Nancy suddenly went all confident and critical.

'Well!' she said. 'Does that include roast potatoes and vegetables or do we have to order them separately and pay lots more money?'

Vixen swung round on her heel and went back to the bar. There were two people she could ask: a man in glasses and a claret-coloured cardigan and a young-ish woman with very flounced, very blonded hair. Vixen eyed them both but neither of them smiled so she chose the man because he was nearer.

'Excuse me,' she said politely—and he still didn't smile—'but do you get vegetables automatically with the—'

'Of course!' he snapped before she could finish.

Feeling quite upset, she made her way back to the table.

'Yes, vegetables do come with it,' she said.

'And potatoes?' asked Nancy, sharp and relentless.

'Oh, I can't go back again!' cried Vixen. 'They're so unfriendly!'

Nancy looked at her oddly.

'Oh, Mum, of course potatoes will come with it,' said Douglas, taking over. 'Now what does everyone want? I'll go and order.'

Vixen sat down thankfully.

'The lamb,' said Nancy.

'Chicken,' said Vixen.

Douglas went off to the bar, word-perfect and bearing his mother's purse.

Obviously feeling slightly more relaxed, Nancy looked around at the decor. It was as if she were seeing it for the first time.

'Haven't you been here before?' asked Vixen curiously.

'Not for years and years,' said Nancy. 'They had wooden tables then, not these beaten copper things. And I bet in the winter they don't have a real fire in that grate any more. They probably have those gas things that look like flames but don't give off any heat.'

Vixen glanced at a particularly nasty painting of an artificial flower arrangement. Even in pictures, the flowers couldn't be real . . .

Douglas came back with three lots of cutlery in paper napkins and a plastic basket of little individual packets.

'What are those?' asked Nancy, wrinkling her nose and all ready to take exception.

'Our condiments,' said Douglas.

They all sifted through them—white packets of salt; brown packets of pepper; splodges of tomato ketchup trapped in plastic.

'Well!' said Nancy. 'They might at least have salt and pepper mills—or even ready-ground in pots if the mills are too much trouble.'

When the meats arrived, they were served with boiled potatoes and peas. Douglas got one limp Yorkshire pudding as well because he was having beef.

'No roast potatoes!' cried Nancy. 'That's shocking for a Sunday!'

Then she took a mouthful of peas.

'Tinned,' she said when her mouth was empty again.

Then she tasted the gravy:

'An Oxo cube,' she said. 'No meat juices.'

Vixen reflected that for people who were really good cooks themselves, eating out was often not much of a pleasure. Which was probably why she never ate out with her father but always did with her mother.

A little later, in search of the Ladies, Vixen found herself going upstairs. As it turned out, there were six or seven people in the bar up there—but not all in one group.

Vixen looked around the room, startled because the decor here was completely different from downstairs. The tables and chairs were an eclectic mix, but all very nice old wooden ones. The pictures on the walls were interesting-looking prints, some of them quite elaborately framed. She recognized one of the customers—it was the 'lady sketch artist' with the piled-up hair; she was sitting at a table by the window, looking down on the street and sketching it. It's much nicer up here, thought Vixen. I'll try and get Nancy and Douglas to move . . .

But on her way out again, she saw someone else she recognized which riveted her to the floor for a moment, looking. Sitting right up close to the bar, a huge wine glass in front of her and leaning her head on her hand, was Alice, Douglas's Lady in the Wood. Vixen got into a panic for some reason and wanted to sneak out without being seen—but, before she could move, Alice had raised her ravaged, bloodshot eyes and was looking straight at her . . . or was she? Vixen looked over her shoulder and nearly jumped out of her skin. On the wall directly behind her was a glass case with a stuffed fox in it. She had seen this kind of thing in country pubs before but that didn't help. Alice had her grey eyes penetratingly fixed on the fox—and then on the vixen. There was no recognition in her expression—just a fixation. Vixen fled.

'What's the matter?' cried Dougie as she appeared back at their beaten-copper table. Her eyes were nearly as wild as Alice's had been.

'There's a dead fox up there!'

'What?'

'I mean a stuffed one. In a glass case.'

'They do have them in pubs round here,' said Nancy. 'It's the country. They have birds as well. And fish.'

'But the fox bothers her, doesn't it?' Douglas explained more sensitively. 'She's a vixen, isn't she?'

'Oh . . . I see,' said Nancy and worriedly looked at Vixen as if she thought she should be tested for madness.

'Let's go,' said Douglas.

'Yes please,' said Vixen. 'This place may be called The Old Red Fox but they prefer their foxes dead.'

They left the remains of their uninspiring dinners and made for the door. The cutlery was left all anyhow on the plates which showed what a rush Vixen had put them all in. Neither Nancy nor Douglas would dream of doing that normally. On one of the plates, a pea was forlornly jammed against a fork-prong. As they were passing the bar, Vixen could almost have sworn that there was another roasted message put in after the original three on the blackboard:

ROAST BEEF
ROAST LAMB
ROAST CHICKEN
ROAST FOX

but she didn't stop to double-check.

'Don't be silly!' said Dougie when she told him outside. 'You can't eat fox!'

Then she remembered her dad talking about something by Oscar Wilde that was on at his theatre: there was a line about fox-hunting referring to 'the unspeakable in pursuit of the uneatable' or something like that.

Their 'treat' for the day had not been a great success: that evening, Nancy, maybe still feeling guilty, cooked them another dinner—and this one was very good; even better than the dinner she served for the boarders first.

Vixen and Dougie sat on either side of the kitchen table with a large blue candle burning between them. Nancy wouldn't sit down and eat with them but insisted on running round and serving them like a waitress— which Vixen didn't feel happy about at all. She didn't know what Douglas was feeling; he was used to his mother after all, used to being treated like a little god. It was a wonder that he didn't stomp around like a complete spoilt brat, but he didn't.

Vixen hoped that this last gesture would settle any remainder of guilt that Nancy still had and leave her free to get into another bad mood if she felt the need.

With her mouth full of iceberg lettuce from the garden and exquisitely hand-done croutons, Vixen wondered again if her father and Nancy could get on. This was the kind of thing he liked.

The sauce for the salmon had chives in it from the herb plot and the home-made strawberry mousse was so wreathed in mint leaf and lemon balm, it was like eating a still-life painting.

After all the courses, Vixen felt so overcome with good food and gratitude that she felt like repaying the favour. She could suggest to Nancy that she try striking up a correspondence with her father because she thought it might lead to that elusive 'love' that everyone went on about and everyone was supposed to want. And she could apologize to Dougie for not telling him that his friend, Alice, was upstairs in the bar at The Old Red Fox.

But she didn't.

The blue candle had burnt down to half its strength. Douglas carefully blew it out and the whole gathering disbanded.

FOURTEEN

The next time Vixen heard voices at night, it was different. It wasn't children singing—or anyone else singing. It was someone talking—going on and on in a tense and pleading way—and it was a voice she recognized. It was Nancy's.

Oh well, she thought, nothing uncanny about that even though it was very late. And she assumed it was Douglas she was talking to. Vixen lay still for a moment, wondering when Douglas was going to contribute and what it was they were talking about. At one point, Nancy's voice raised up so she could hear the words clearly.

'. . . big house. Father left it me. All very well but I wanted to fill it with children.'

Then another voice answered but it wasn't Douglas's—it was another woman's.

She's got a friend round, thought Vixen in surprise. Why's she come so late—and why are they having an argument?

The friend's voice was lower than Nancy's. Vixen couldn't make out the words but she did vaguely recognize the voice.

She sat up.

A phrase here and there became more clear.

'Can't. Just can't . . . don't suit the life . . . can't bear it again.'

Then Nancy's voice again, sounding almost hysterical.

'You've got it and you don't want it! I've never wanted anything else and I can't seem to get it!'

Then the other voice murmured something about men.

And Nancy snapped, 'Of course there's been men. Well, no, not men. One man once. But I didn't like him!'

Vixen shivered. She was fairly sure by now that the other voice was Alice's—but Alice sounding much younger than she usually did and sober. Maybe the alcohol made your voice crack, thought Vixen, perplexed.

Something must have happened! Alice had come over to say something about Douglas and they were fighting over him. Not that the dialogue she had heard particularly added up to that—but she couldn't think what else it could be. Meanwhile, Douglas, no doubt, was lying asleep in his paisley pyjamas, unaware that his secret friend was revealing herself to his mother.

I ought to warn him, thought Vixen then—and got out of bed. She was wearing a green nightshirt nearly the same colour as the carpet so she moved across the room in a bit of a blur.

But, out on the landing, she stopped dead—nowhere near Dougie's room. Here both voices were audible, floating up so clearly that she thought they must be speaking in the hall. And the second one didn't sound so much like Alice now . . .

Vixen listened to the voice. Then she did something she had never done in her life before: she fled down the stairs, calling 'Mum, Mum, Mum,' suddenly really desperate to see her.

But when she landed in the hall, there was no one there. She stopped dead again, suddenly feeling terribly embarrassed about what she had just done and hoping no one in the house had heard.

And how could it possibly be her mother?! Why on earth would it be?

She could still hear the voices, so now she assumed they were in the living room—in the room that had the blue velvet chair and where Douglas's fox puppet had been lying all askew when she first arrived. The door was shut. Vixen headed straight for it and put her hand on the knob.

But then she hesitated.

What was she doing? She told herself off: you don't just barge in on other people's private conversations! And she shouldn't be listening at the door either!

But now she had come this far, she couldn't move. Torn between guilt and curiosity, she stood in her green nightshirt, her bare feet sinking into the deep patterned carpet, and did what most people would have done and carried on listening.

The tone had changed. There was less hysteria in Nancy's voice now—she sounded as if she was telling a story—and it was all very serious.

'It's been done,' she was saying. 'There's a story connected to this house. Have you ever heard it?'

'I think I might have done,' said the other person cautiously.

'Well, a baby was . . . er . . . sold to the people that lived here then. Some sort of exchange took place anyway. The baby was brought up here and I believe the woman from the village went to foreign parts—just like you want to. Nobody ever knew and—'

'If nobody ever knew,' interrupted the other voice, 'then how come there's a story about it?'

Nancy didn't falter or lose patience.

'I mean, no one ever knew at the time,' she said. 'There's no record of anything disastrous happening to the child so you needn't be superstitious about it and—'

'I am not superstitious.'

Nancy didn't respond for a moment but then said, 'Well then, there's nothing to stop you, is there?'

Vixen couldn't listen to any more without letting them know she was there. She knocked gently on the door.

They merely carried on talking.

She knocked louder.

Still they talked.

Feeling very irritated, she opened the door a crack.

There was still no response to her, so she pushed the door open as wide as it would go and stepped on to the threshold. This took the form of a metal strip which was sharply cold to her feet, so she got off it and took a couple of steps into the room proper.

Absolutely no one there at all.

Panicking, she looked everywhere around—even behind the blue armchair and the damask sofa. The only sounds in the room now were the ticking of the clock on the mantelpiece and her own heart wildly beating.

She did what she had done before when she heard the singing: she rushed round every room on the ground floor, looking. This meant going in and out of the hall all the time and even in a fevered state, she still noticed the unnatural coldness of that space. The handing over of the baby must have taken place here, she thought. That's why it stays so cold.

She was very tempted to wake Douglas up so she wasn't alone with all this, but then remembered that he hadn't heard the voices last time. They seemed to be just for her. Also, it would be mean to disturb him. But, standing there shivering, she knew she had to at least get out of the hall.

She went into the kitchen and stared at the solid-looking vegetable motifs on the wall-tiles. They had seemed so comforting last time she was disturbed in the night. If she had been a child, she would have given them names: Miss Onion and Mr Lettuce and Dr Corn-On-The-Cob and Gregory the Green Cabbage and Ruby the Red Cabbage . . . then her eyes landed on a fat purple beetroot and she shuddered. Beetroot was one of the few things she couldn't eat. But, pausing at this tile, she realized she couldn't hear the voices any more. She sighed with relief. I must have been dreaming, she thought uneasily—knowing full well that she hadn't been. Wearily, almost as if she were very old or in pain, she left the kitchen. The menacing chill of the hall clutched at her again—and then she speeded up. She was halfway up the stairs when the baby started wailing. Then she really bolted. The singing started of course—bang on cue:

'Wind the bobbin up—
Wind the bobbin up . . . '

Vixen knew now that there was no point rushing round all the rooms in search of the singers: she wouldn't find them. And no point waking Douglas up: he wouldn't hear them.

'Wind the bobbin up—
Wind the bobbin up.'

And then a pause in the singing and Nancy's voice saying very clearly:

'I have a friend who's a midwife.'

'Wind it up! Wind, wind . . . '

Pause again.

'No one need ever know but you, me, and her. She's my friend. She'd do it.'

Baby wailing.

'Wind, wind, wind it up . . . '

Vixen put her hands over her ears and ran for her bedroom. She had to take one hand off of course to open the door and then a complete mix of the two things assailed her: the reedy singing of the long-ago children soothing the baby who had been acquired, not born there—and the tense but decisive discussion between Nancy and the other woman. Only this time, all at the same time.

Almost screaming, Vixen half-charged, half-fell into

her bedroom where the dawn was starting to filter through the curtains. She got to the window, flung the curtains apart, and looked down into the garden. Dozens of shadowy baby foxes were cavorting on the lawn, vague as ghosts but clear enough to Vixen.

FIFTEEN

She went with Dougie to see Alice in the wood again less than five hours later. She was in a sort of haunted trance by now and hadn't even begun to think what she was going to do about it. She let Dougie lead her through the fields; usually they kept pace with each other or she was in front. He stopped and turned round before they got to the wood.

'Are you all right?' he asked, peering at her curiously.

Vixen automatically started to say 'Yes thank you', but trailed off before the end because it wasn't true. Dougie wasn't an adult she had to be polite to.

'Did you . . . er . . . hear things again last night?' he asked.

'Yes I did,' she said at once. No point in beating about the bush even though he never heard things himself.

'And saw things,' she added.

'The foxes again?'

She nodded.

'You must be going to uncover a big secret,' said Douglas earnestly.

Vixen wondered, quite seriously now, what it was going to be.

Just before they reached the glade, they heard the sound of a hacking cough.

'Poor Alice,' said Douglas with concern—and they went into the sunlight from the shade.

Alice was on her log again, silky dress sweeping over the patches of moss. As soon as she opened her mouth to greet them, Vixen thought, She's drunk, but Dougie just didn't seem to notice. He did his usual fussing round her arranging things which Alice took as totally her due. This time the tartan rug she was sitting on was sombre. The last one had had a lot of deep blue in it—this one was the much plainer Black Watch.

'Tired of this place,' said Alice fretfully. 'Too hot in the sun.' And she coughed again.

'Would you like to go somewhere else?' asked Dougie politely.

Alice looked at him with eyes that were very wide open for a moment. Vixen found herself thinking of Little Red Riding Hood for some reason— 'Grandmother, Grandmother, what big eyes you have . . . ' In that case, of course, the grandmother was a wolf in a bonnet.

'Yes,' said Alice in answer to Dougie's question. 'I want you to come and see me in my house. It's cooler there.' Then her lids half closed and her glance was veiled again. She pulled the brim of her hat down lower.

A great feeling of danger came sweeping over Vixen but Douglas was just blithely saying, 'Oh yes. When shall we come?'

'Count me out!' whispered Vixen fiercely—but then realized she couldn't possibly let him go on his own . . .

'Tomorrow,' said Alice. Her voice was cracked but certain. 'Tomorrow. Come for tea at four o'clock.'

'Oh thank you,' said Douglas. 'But where? I don't know your address.'

'Well . . . ' began Alice.

'I'm . . . er . . . just going for a walk,' said Vixen suddenly.

The desire to get away was overpowering. Maybe a fox just couldn't stay for long in the same place as a wolf.

'All right then. See you later,' said Douglas placidly— but Alice just turned and stared at her, keeping her bloodshot eyes fixed on Vixen while she beat her retreat.

It was only because she had another coughing fit that she stopped.

Vixen struck into a direction she hadn't taken before. The path through this part of the woods was clearly marked so she found herself running.

'Wolf, wolf . . . ' she said through her teeth. 'Must get away from the wolf . . . '

And then she was brought up short by the 'lady sketch artist' sitting right in the way. Vixen skidded but didn't crash into her.

The artist turned her wheat-coloured head. She was sitting on a little stool, the sort that you collapse and carry under your arm. She and Vixen looked at each other for a moment.

'Why aren't you out of breath?' asked the artist with interest. 'You've been running but you're not out of breath.'

'I'm used to running,' said Vixen. Her eyes were gleaming and her hair looked very red even in the dimness under the trees.

'What are you drawing?' she asked.

'That,' said the artist and pointed to the ground in front of her.

Vixen bent down and saw a clump of toadstools with deep reddish-brown caps and bone-white stalks. There was a big one and a cluster of much smaller ones round its base.

'It's like a parent with children, isn't it?' said the artist.

'Yes,' said Vixen, straightening again. She was interested to note that the artist said 'parent' and not automatically 'mother' like a lot of other people might have done at the sight of clustering babies round a bigger organism. Maybe she too had been brought up by her father . . .

'A completely poisonous little family,' said the artist peacefully.

Vixen was quite startled at this allusion until she remembered they were talking about toadstools.

'You might bump into the major if you carry on running in the wood,' said the artist.

'The major?'

'You know—one of the other boarders at The House. His great-nephew has come down to see him for the day.'

'Great-nephew?' said Vixen, thinking how ponderous that sounded. 'Not grandson?'

'Oh no,' said the artist as if she were absolutely certain. 'The major hasn't got any children, so he wouldn't have grandchildren, would he?'

She hummed gently as she sketched in the final baby toadstool.

'Neither have I,' she added.

'Neither have you what?' asked Vixen.

'Got any children,' she said serenely—and started to attend to the finer details of her poisonous picture.

'Er . . . see you later,' said Vixen. 'At The House maybe?'

'Oh yes,' said the artist.

Vixen skirted her collapsible stool (on the opposite side to the toadstools) and struck deeper into the wood.

At one point, she wanted sunlight again like someone under water craving air. She left the path and went off to the side, picking her way carefully over the thorns and big leaves and fungi. She came to a fence and leaned out over it. A big green field stretched in front of her and, at the far side of it, she saw the 'retired gentleman' from The House, striding along with a stick in his hand and a big floppy hat—almost like a jungle hat—on his head. Walking next to him was a little boy, younger than Douglas, dressed in baggy khaki shorts, a navy blue T-shirt, and a miniature version of his great-uncle's hat. Vixen took as much as she needed of the sunshine, and then returned to the trees.

She left the path again eventually—because she felt like it—but thicker into the woods this time not up to the fields. Suddenly, completely without warning, she came upon two other people. She had come into a small clearing in the trees which had the effect of a murky little lair. The two people were a youngish man and woman and Vixen instantly knew they were the 'young couple' from The House even though she had never met them before.

They were sitting on the broad swinging branch of a huge tree which was the main focal point in the lair. They both looked in Vixen's direction but there was something wild and primitive about their glance as if she had dredged them up from something very deep and basic. She also detected the faint flavour of resentment at being disturbed. She shivered slightly and moved on.

But the look in their eyes haunted her. She somehow knew that if she looked back at them, they wouldn't be sitting on the branch any more. They'd be sprawling on the ground. The image of a wailing baby floated in her mind.

Vixen had a sudden desire to be out of the wood: her sense of direction tended to be very good and she was soon tearing across the field that led to the road that led to The House. She knew she was going very fast—it was never any effort to her—but she couldn't notice if she was enjoying it very much. Her mind was too set on doing one thing. Everything seemed to be on her side so she didn't have to stop running and mess about with things.

The big gate to the driveway was open so she just ran through it and even the front door of The House was open so she skidded off the gravel straight over the threshold and into the hall. Nancy was passing through on her way to another room—and she jumped violently at Vixen's entrance. She didn't drop any of the things she was carrying though.

'You look as if a pack of hounds were after you!' she remarked.

Vixen shuddered at this, then smiled vaguely to be polite, and made for the payphone which was set up in the hall for the boarders. Nancy conveniently went into the living room and shut the door.

Vixen dialled her father's number, hurtled the coins into the slot and waited, quivering, for him to answer.

He wasn't there—she got the answer machine.

She waited impatiently for the tone, then recklessly poured her worries into the receiver.

'Dad—remember that strange woman I told you about in the wood? The one that's got some sort of hold over Douglas? Well, I thought it was safe enough seeing her in the wood—sort-of, anyway. But now she wants us to go to her house. Tomorrow at four. And I don't feel so safe about that. It'll be like going into her lair—and she'll have more power there than in the wood . . . Dougie will go though—it's almost like she can compel him to do anything. So I'll have to go too—in case it's dangerous—but I think she could have power over me too if I'm not careful. There's something about her and—'

Nancy came out of the living room and Vixen put the phone down at once.

Sixteen

Alice's house was a similar size and of similar age and of the same stone as Nancy's—but much simpler in design. It was also much more dilapidated.

'This would have been magnificent once,' said Douglas in his oddly grown-up way. He and Vixen were marching up Alice's driveway. There were huge rhododendron bushes on either side of them.

'Not as magnificent as your mum's,' said Vixen.

Douglas didn't reply to that. Vixen peered at him curiously: he had that obstinate, pursed-lip look about him again. There was no doubt about it—he was very drawn to Alice in some inexplicable way.

Behind the glass at the top of the front door, two porcelain King Charles spaniels sat back to back. One of them had a chipped ear. Vixen had her eyes on the dogs when Alice opened the door—but a distinct flash of unexpected red made her look down immediately.

Alice was wearing a full-length red velvet dress and a string of pearls. Her grey hair was done in a French pleat; pearl earrings on small chains were hanging from her ears and a half-empty glass was hanging from her hand.

Vixen stared at her, completely astonished.

'Oh, Alice!' cried Douglas. 'You look lovely!'

Vixen said nothing. She was thinking more along the lines of, How ridiculous for this time of day.

'Come in, come in!' said Alice—which sounded friendly enough—but she still fixed Vixen with a penetrating glare. Her hall was lined with pictures of fox-hunting scenes, framed in gilt. This was no surprise to Vixen.

Rather unsteadily, Alice led them to what she called the 'parlour'. This was a huge room with at least two of its pictures hanging crooked. Douglas immediately went over and straightened them. Vixen gasped—but then thought he could probably get away with it. Anyway, he was like her father: he would rather risk annoying Alice than sit in a room with crooked pictures.

The furniture was mainly stiff and rigid, but there was one voluptuous, soft armchair which looked more modern than the other things and which Alice now sank into. She was still holding the glass, which was now empty, and she carelessly waved it in the direction of something which Vixen would have identified as a mustard-coloured Victorian morning sofa—having seen so many of them labelled in junk shops. Vixen and Douglas took Alice's gesture to mean 'sit on that', which they did—side by side like visiting urchins being granted favours.

Douglas was to be offered more favours than Vixen though.

'Would you like a drink, Douglas, my dear?' slurred Alice, putting her empty glass down and picking up a bottle of wine, mostly drunk.

'No thank you,' said Douglas cheerfully. 'But shall I make a cup of tea for us all?'

Alice's expression told that she found this a completely ridiculous suggestion but then she was shaken by a coughing fit, which made it just as well that the bottle she was holding was almost empty. Douglas got up from the morning sofa, gently took the bottle from her and handed it to Vixen, who was very tempted to swig straight out of it but refrained because it hadn't been offered to her and she didn't want to arouse Alice's wrath. In that moment, Vixen could completely understand why people drink to deal with their frazzled nerves.

Douglas went round every chair and sofa in the room (there were quite a few of them), garnering cushions. He propped them all up behind Alice's back saying, 'Poor Alice. You'll be better soon.'

I wonder, thought Vixen, eyeing her curiously.

Alice, for the moment, looked defeated. She leaned back against the cushions, wheezing; the lids closed over the bloodshot eyes and it was rather alarming.

'It's all right,' said Douglas. 'She's just resting. I'll find the kitchen and make tea.'

'Silver pot,' Alice suddenly croaked. 'And tea strainer in the drawer.' She kept her eyes shut though.

When Douglas went to the kitchen, a great stillness seemed to fall upon the parlour. Vixen sat as if glued to the morning sofa, still clutching hold of the wine bottle.

Douglas reappeared, complete with tray, three cups and saucers, a small jug of milk, sugar lumps in a silver dish—sugar tongs carefully balanced on top of them; tea-strainer and a very tarnished silver teapot. At least one of the cups had a chip in it and the milk jug was cracked. Douglas made a real show of pouring out the tea and handing out the cups. He put Alice's on the little table next to her chair. She ignored it. Suddenly, she began to talk but it was all disjointed sentences and croaking fragments.

'Thought I saw William again today. Not in that white thing though. In his jacket again. And tie . . . '

'She's rambling,' Vixen whispered to Douglas.

'Shush!' he said. He was listening to Alice as if she was talking to him direct.

'Told him about the money . . . Money gone, money all gone . . . '

Unexpectedly, Alice sat up on the edge of the chair, opened her eyes wide, looked straight at Douglas and smiled.

He smiled back, completely trusting.

Can't he see that she's mad? thought Vixen. The feeling of being in Alice's lair was drawing tighter and tighter. They mustn't stay too long, they mustn't . . .

'Nice boy,' said Alice coaxingly. 'You'd like to live here with me, wouldn't you?'

Vixen jumped to her feet at this, all prepared to just drag him away.

'Sit down, Vixen!' said Douglas crossly. 'You're not being polite!'

'But . . . but . . . ' stammered Vixen, and then found herself caught in Alice's predatory grey stare as well. She sat down again.

'Not sure about you,' said Alice. 'Had a girl before . . . things didn't work out with the girl. She . . . ' then she wrinkled her forehead as if trying to remember something.

Vixen looked at Douglas who was gazing at Alice. Maybe she's hypnotizing him, she thought.

Alice got up, walked over to the morning sofa and abruptly jammed herself in between the two of them. A fold of the red velvet dress fell across Vixen's legs. It was so heavy that it made her panic—she flung it away before it could hold her down. Even more of the dress had fallen in Douglas's direction. There was so much material in it that it was covering him like a curtain. Vixen hastily leaned across to pull it off him—but a thin, spidery hand seized her wrist.

'Some people like the feel of old velvet,' said Alice, gripping Vixen's hand so hard it hurt.

'Well I do myself!' cried Vixen. 'But I don't like it smothering me! And I'm sure Douglas doesn't either!'

She grabbed at the velvet with her other hand, but Douglas said, 'It feels so rich and soft and I love the colour.' He was stroking the stuff like you would a cat.

'Dougie!' said Vixen. 'I think we should go home now!'

'And how will you do that?' enquired Alice with interest.

'Same way as we got in! Through the door!'

'Oh,' said Alice, and the frightening thing was that she sounded completely clear and unconfused now. 'Well, I'm afraid that there's rather a curious device on my front door. It keeps us all safely locked in—and only I know how to work it. It makes sense, you see. It wouldn't be right for people to just come and go as they like when it's my house, would it?'

Vixen ran straight out of the room, through the hall with the hunting scenes and up to the front door. But no matter how much she pushed and pulled at all the handles and catches, the door wouldn't open. The back door, the back door, she feverishly thought and ran with no compunction through all the rooms until she got to it. But that was locked as well, of course. She looked wildly round for a key but couldn't see one anywhere. We'll just have to climb out of a window, she thought, and rushed back to the parlour to get Douglas. And if the windows are all locked, we'll break one. We'll have to. It won't be an offence. We've got to get out.

When she got to the parlour, there had been another change. The little table that was standing by Alice's soft armchair had now been moved to the morning sofa. Alice and Douglas were sitting on either side of it and Alice was laying out the intricate pieces of an old-fashioned-looking board game. Vixen was transfixed by it for a moment in spite of wanting to get out: it was so much more elaborate and extravagantly painted than a modern one would be. Even from where she was standing, she could make out the varied shapes: cherubs with much bigger wings than they usually have; travellers in cloaks and big boots with packs on their backs; imposing figures waving pitchfork things—she couldn't make out whether these were devils or gardeners—and there were assorted animals in clothes doing human things, including the inevitable foxes. She got closer to the board. The dog foxes were dressed in scarlet hunting jackets and white breeches and the vixens in green Victorian riding habits! Seeing the foxes like that was a great delight and Vixen almost relented and asked if she could play too . . . but then she heard Alice telling Douglas the rules of the game. There was something gloating about her voice and the game sounded rather nasty—although afterwards, Vixen could not have said what you had to do . . . But she looked at Alice's unnatural stare fixed on Douglas and Douglas's rapt attention—and alarm bells sounded in her head again.

'Dougie,' she said. 'We ought to go.'

'Don't be ridiculous!' snapped Alice so abruptly that Vixen jumped. 'We've only just begun the game. And anyway, Dougie's not going home any more. He's staying here with me!'

At that, Vixen just seized hold of Douglas. She was fairly strong and he came right off the sofa, but he was struggling.

'No, Vixen!' he cried. 'I want to play this board game!'

'You'll be playing more than a board game if you stay here,' said Vixen grimly, and started to drag him towards the nearest window. She didn't know what else to do.

'You're a fox dragging an innocent chicken away,' Alice suddenly remarked. She had produced another drink as if from nowhere and was watching them.

'Unlock the front door for us!' cried Vixen furiously. But even at a time like that, her up-bringing conquered and she added 'Please,' which put a lame end to the demand.

Alice laughed, and it was such a laugh that Vixen jumped again, really startled. Even Douglas stopped struggling and stared uneasily at his idol. Cackle, cackle, cackle she went—rising to a crescendo. She sounded like a banshee; like a witch; like one of those menacing toys that you wind up and leave to do its stuff . . .

Vixen and Douglas were frozen to the floor, Vixen still hanging on to Douglas's arm. The highly-painted board game was between them and Alice. One of the devil-gardeners had fallen on top of a cherub and, as they looked, one of the foxes toppled too—but she went right off the board, scooping the cherub with her but not the devil-gardener.

Then suddenly there was another element. Somebody else dashed into the room and cried, 'Mother, what are you doing to these children?'

Vixen felt a rushing in the ears and a spinning of the head at the sound of that voice. No, no, it can't be, she thought in amazement—but she turned round and yes, it was: it was her own mother! She nearly dropped to the floor with the shock of it. Douglas cried, 'Who are you?' but the most astounded of all was Alice.

She fell back on to the sofa, spilling the contents of the glass, and it brought an abrupt end to the laughter. Laura Thomas adroitly twitched the glass out of her hand before it could do damage.

'You . . . you . . .' gasped Alice. She turned her wild eyes on Douglas. 'This is the . . . the girl. The other girl. It didn't work out. She—' But then she stopped speaking and went blue in the face with coughing.

Laura turned at once to Douglas but she didn't really look at him.

'Is Doctor Murray still practising in the village?' she asked quietly. Her initial alarm had quite vanished.

'Yes,' said Douglas. 'He's my doctor. And my mum's. But . . .'

'Don't ask now,' said Laura—and this time, she did look at him, and it was very oddly. 'Your gra— I mean . . . Alice needs him. Can you run and get him, please?'

Vixen found her tongue.

'He can't get out! There's a special thing on the front door!'

Laura smiled rather grimly. 'Oh, I'll deal with that!' she said.

She strode out into the hall with both Vixen and Douglas at her heels. She did something to the catch on the front door—too swiftly for them to see what—and opened it.

Douglas immediately ran up the front path to go and get help for his friend.

Vixen and Laura looked at each other.

'How did you get in?' asked Vixen.

'With my own key,' said Laura. 'I haven't used it for years, of course—but I hadn't lost it. I wondered if she might have changed the locks. But she hasn't.'

'But what about the device?'

'It only works from the inside. You can still get in with a key from the outside.'

'And . . . and how did you know to come? And—'

'We must get back to mother,' said Laura gently—and they returned to the parlour.

'But . . . but . . . ' Vixen was still stammering—and not surprisingly.

'Don't ask any questions for a bit, Vixen,' said Laura. 'We've got work to do.' And she started seeing to Alice even more efficiently than Douglas did. She was directing and involving Vixen too.

'Beat all those cushions so that she's half sitting up. Then she'll breathe more easily. Get her a glass of water. Let's get her shoes off . . . '

It didn't occur to Vixen to do anything other than

obey her mother. It seemed for those few minutes as if Laura was the wisest, most enlightened person in the world. When Alice looked a lot more comfortable and her eyes were half closed as if she meant to sleep, Laura said, 'Vixen, meet your grandmother.'

Vixen just stared.

'You've met her once before. But you were a baby so you probably won't remember.'

Laura then sat down in the armchair. Now she was still, the usual atmosphere of haunted trouble came over her. Vixen felt as if she could almost touch it. She sat down herself.

'This is the house I was brought up in,' said Laura. 'I . . .'

'So I did come to your village after all,' said Vixen in a daze.

Alice suddenly stirred and muttered. She turned her glittering gaze on Laura for a moment—then closed her eyes again.

'How could you . . . how could you?' she was saying.

'How could I what, mother?' asked Laura clearly.

'Leave him. Leave him.'

Vixen bit her lip. She didn't need to be told that they were talking about her father.

'William meant so much to me!' cried Alice weakly.

'I didn't though, did I?' said Laura—but completely without resentment. She said it almost humorously.

'You were . . . you were . . . ' stumbled Alice.

'You didn't like having a daughter, did you?' said Laura still in the same tone. 'You sent me away as soon as you could.'

'It . . . it . . . was best . . . '

'Yes, maybe it was,' mused Laura. But then she looked at her own daughter and her face was full of pain. Vixen didn't move or speak but her eyes filled.

107

There was a frantic knocking on the front door and Laura got up at once.

'There's more, mother,' she said sadly. 'I've been much worse than you know.'

She went to open the door and ushered in the doctor and Douglas.

The first thing the doctor said was, 'Laura! How long must it be since I've seen you? It must be . . . '

'Twelve years,' said Laura with an odd look at Douglas. Vixen saw the look and didn't understand it—and Dougie was only concerned with what was happening to Alice.

While the doctor was seeing to her, the other three sat in the kitchen. It wasn't comfortable in there. Vixen sat on a chair which needed a lot of concentration because the legs slithered sideways from the seat in strange, snake-like movements. Laura was perched on a high stool uneasily swinging her long legs like a teenager. Dougie sat on the lowest chair of all and was completely pensive and silent. Vixen had never seen him like that before. Laura kept biting her lip and looking at him. Vixen kept trying to ask questions but Laura didn't seem to want to talk in front of Douglas. Vixen got beyond the stage of shock and pity and wanted just to bang their heads together. She kept making tea and giving Douglas the biggest mug hoping to send him running for the bathroom. In the end, it worked. Laura told him where it was (or, as she put it, where it always used to be) and he was barely through the door before Vixen launched herself.

'How did you know to come?' she cried. 'How on earth did you know?'

Laura hesitated.

'Quick, he'll be back in a minute!' Vixen almost screamed.

'Well . . . I dropped in at your flat not knowing you

were away and your father told me you were but still asked me in—'

'Well, of course he would!' interrupted Vixen indignantly.

'And . . . and then he saw he had a message on the answer machine—so he played it back and it was that one from you saying how agitated you were about . . . about . . . the strange woman in the wood and coming here for tea.'

For tea, thought Vixen. What a laugh!

'Don't ask me how . . . but I knew you must be talking about my mother. Your grandmother! And then Kevin told me the name of the village and that confirmed it!'

'But wasn't it the most amazing coincidence?' cried Vixen. 'There must be loads of villages in the Cotswolds! Why did I end up in the one you came from? Dad never came here with you, did he?'

'No—and he only met my mother once, and that was in London when she came to see you as a baby. And she's certainly changed beyond all recognition now. He wanted to come with me today, of course—but I begged and begged him to let me handle it alone. I knew I finally had to confront my mother, you see, and . . . and other things.'

Vixen raised her eyebrows at this but Laura didn't enlighten her. She hoped she would find out later and:

'How did you get here?' she asked next.

'Went straight to Paddington—got the next train to Worcester and then a cab from there.'

There was an abrupt pause.

And then Vixen couldn't help going back to the wonder of the coincidence:

'So how could I end up here? I think Nana was worried that I might—and then decided that it was too unlikely. Like winning the lottery.'

Laura looked embarrassed and then came out with something not typical of her at all:

'Well . . . er . . . maybe there is no such thing as a coincidence,' she said, blushing at her own unlikely words. After all, the notion of 'Fate' was much more up Vixen's street than hers. 'Not many things stay secret for ever, do they?'

Vixen looked taken aback.

'But . . . but whether you believe in coincidence or not,' she said, 'there's Douglas too. He had become friends with . . . my grandmother . . . ' she stumbled over that term—she wasn't used to it. 'That's extraordinary!'

Laura looked at her with an expression she couldn't begin to read.

'Well,' she said, 'that's one thing that isn't a coincidence at all . . . '

'But—' began Vixen—and then Douglas came back in the room, followed very closely by the doctor.

The doctor looked grave.

'Could I have a word with you alone please, Laura?' he asked.

Silently, she followed him out of the kitchen and shut the door.

'Alice is going to die, isn't she?' said Douglas woodenly to Vixen. But then he burst into tears.

The doctor's wife was a very experienced nurse. They arranged that she and Laura would watch over Alice all night, taking it in turns. She took first turn.

Laura insisted on taking Douglas and Vixen home. Douglas didn't resist, although he remained miserable and stubborn-looking.

'It's this way,' he said at one point.

'It's all right thank you, Douglas,' said Laura. 'I know it like the back of my hand.'

'Are you friends with my mum then?' he asked.

'Er . . . sort of,' she said.

But when they were approaching the driveway, she faltered. She seemed uncertain whether to take them up it or not.

'We'll be all right now,' said Douglas, tight-lipped and trying to take over.

Vixen didn't know what to do at all. She had a strong and unaccustomed feeling that she didn't want her mother to leave her.

'I'll . . . I'll just see you halfway up,' said Laura. 'Does the house still look the same?'

'You'll see if you come halfway up,' said Douglas drily.

Laura flashed him a glance, nearly said something—but then didn't.

Their three pairs of shoes were scrunching up the gravel—but they weren't talking. Before they were quite halfway, something unexpected happened. The front door opened and out came Nancy. She looked at them for a moment, startled. Her eyes lingered the longest over Laura and then a big change came over her. Vixen couldn't decide whether she was going to laugh or scream. What she did was nearer the latter.

'You promised you'd never come back!' she cried.

Laura looked as if she was going to bolt, but then steadied herself.

'It's all right, Nancy,' she said. 'I'm only dropping these two off. Look after them please. They've had a shock.'

She turned to go but Nancy said 'Wait!' really sharply. 'Get in the house please, Douglas,' she said to her son. And he was too miserable to do anything but obey.

Nancy came forward and caught hold of Laura's arm. Vixen could tell that her mother was dying to shake it off again, but didn't. Nancy was frantic.

'What have you told him?' she demanded. 'What does he know?'

Laura looked straight into Nancy's eyes.

'Nothing at all,' she said—and turned on her heel.

Nancy was left staring after her.

Vixen stood like a stone for a moment and then bounded after Laura.

'I want to come with you,' she said to her.

Laura smiled.

'Thank you,' she said.

SEVENTEEN

No other words passed between them until they were walking side by side up Alice's driveway. Then, 'I'm hungry,' said Laura simply. She had just dealt with near-hysterics and shock in other people and her mother was probably going to die—and 'I'm hungry,' was all she had to say at this point. And yet, in her, it didn't seem sacrilegious or only thinking about herself. Vixen was beginning to wonder if her mother could get away with anything.

The doctor's wife heard them coming into the hall and emerged to meet them.

'She's sleeping now,' she whispered. 'I'm quite happy to stay longer if you want to sort yourselves out a bit.'

'I'll just look at her,' said Laura and disappeared into the parlour while Vixen was left staring with a kind of fascinated horror at one of the hunting pictures. It was called 'The Blooding'.

When Laura came back out, she found her daughter pale and shaky and biting her lip. Laura looked at the picture and then coolly took it off the wall. She turned it round and propped it against the skirting board.

'Come on, Foxy,' said Laura. 'You need food.'

But the valiant attempt at light-heartedness was not going to last long, they both knew that.

With Laura, 'food' always meant not doing it yourself, so Vixen automatically opened the front door. There wasn't likely to be anything much in Alice's kitchen anyway!

As they were approaching the village, Vixen realized there would be a problem.

'There's only English food here,' she said. 'Just roast beef and things. Well, it was on Sunday anyway.'

'I would love some roast beef,' said Laura.

'You would? But it's so English!'

Laura gave her a strange little smile. 'So?'

'Are you starting to be more interested in England then?' asked Vixen incredulously.

'Something like that,' said Laura. 'But I'm not sure it will work.'

They were now in sight of the three pubs: The Three Travellers, The Kings Arms, and The Old Red Fox.

'Not The Old Red Fox, please,' said Vixen in a sudden panic. 'We were there on Sunday and I didn't like it.'

Laura glanced at her but didn't ask any questions.

'Not The Three Travellers either then,' she said. 'I want to get away from myself tonight. Let's go to The Kings Arms. That suggests enough of solid, old-fashioned England, doesn't it?'

But The Kings Arms didn't do food. And neither did The Three Travellers. They were both so hungry that Vixen resigned herself to facing The Old Red Fox after all.

There was nothing roasted on the chalk board tonight. Obviously that only happened on Sundays.

'Shepherd's pie?' suggested Laura. 'Can't get more English than that.'

But Vixen shuddered. 'If there's one thing I can't eat,' she said, 'it's mashed potato.' Then she found herself adding: 'If you'd been around more, you would have known that.' She could have bitten her tongue off the moment she'd said it because Laura's face was instantly full of guilt and pain.

Not that that was anything new.

They ended up asking for fish and chips and went in search of a table.

Laura wanted to go upstairs and Vixen had to steel

herself to get past the glass case with the stuffed, dead fox in it. She was going to point it out but then remembered her mother had removed the painting that bothered her in her grandmother's hallway. Maybe she would smash the glass case and Vixen was too intimidated by the pub already to risk that.

There were about a dozen people up there—some sitting at tables eating and some at the bar. Almost as one, they all stared at Vixen and Laura and kept it up all the time they were crossing the floor and establishing themselves at a table by the window. When Vixen bent down to fasten an erring shoelace, she felt the eyes boring into her and when Laura rolled up her shirt sleeves because she was hot, the whole room was looking at her tanned arms with the watch on the wrist of one and the African bangle on the wrist of the other.

'Hang on a minute,' said Vixen desperately to her mother. 'If they want to stare, I'll give them something to stare at.'

She waited to be stopped as you would expect most parents to do—but Laura was merely looking interested. So Vixen got off her chair, knelt on the floor, and stood on her head. Laura went into the most gratifying peal of laughter—and at last the eyes in the room turned away. There was a lot of muttering and clicking and a nervous giggle from someone fairly young but the staring ceased. For the time being anyway. Canned fifties music suddenly started up and it was just at the right volume; loud enough so that you could feel more private from everyone around you but not so loud that you couldn't have a conversation with the person you were with.

And here, against the unlikely background of fifties dance music, with chips and cod and chunky half-moons of lemons on the table between them, Laura told Vixen some things she had never heard before—or had only heard sketchily. While they talked, the room seemed to close in on them more and more. At one point, Vixen was convinced that the ceiling was getting lower. She looked up fearfully and was sure that the light shade was swinging although Laura said it wasn't.

Laura's parents had been absolutely mad about each other which, as she said, may sound very romantic but it meant there was no room for anyone else—which was tough if you were their child.

'I was an accident, of course,' said Laura.

So was I, thought Vixen.

'I was sent to boarding school when I was eight—and it felt like a prison. Mind you, I think home would have done as well. That's when I first knew I wanted to be a traveller.'

She went on to the bit then that Vixen knew more about: how she had gone to university in London and Kevin Courtney had been working in the bookshop where she went all the time and they had got to know each other, had assumed that they were in love and then decided to get married and go travelling together—and how Laura had been obsessed with it and Kevin had realized after quite a short time that he hated it. And how they had only stopped because Laura was pregnant and he had persuaded her to settle in one place and she found that she couldn't stand it and had to go off again.

'It wasn't the two of you I couldn't stand!' said Laura. 'It was just the having to be in one place and be domestic. You needn't think that I haven't been consumed with guilt about it every day of my life since.'

'But we've been all right,' said Vixen defensively. 'Me and Dad.'

There was a big pause then. Laura's lip was trembling. She leant her face on her hand and stared down at the table—which was made melancholy by the squeezed lemons strewn about on the anaemic white plates.

116

Vixen turned her head sharply because she had a sudden notion of the fox coming out of its case and creeping into the room to find who had killed it. She also saw that the room was emptying—only half the people were left now.

Laura abruptly started again as if she knew she had to get it over with.

'When I first left you, I went to my mother's,' she said. 'That was terrible. I knew she would have been devastated by the death of my father but I thought she would have begun to get over it by then. He died when I was at college. She was drinking heavily and all her money had been squandered on God knows what. We never got on, me and your grandmother, but I would have tried to help in some way. She rounded on me, though. She ordered me away and asked how anyone could bear to leave their husband.'

No mention of child though, thought Vixen wryly.

'And . . . and . . . then . . . ' Suddenly Laura started faltering in her tale as if she was sifting through things in her mind and maybe leaving bits out. 'Then . . . then I went to see Nancy who was someone I knew living just outside the village and . . . and . . . she ended up lending me some money. She lent me enough for a plane fare and enough to live on for a few weeks while I looked for work.'

'And what did you do for her?' asked Vixen sharply. Into her mind had come unbidden her strange ghostly experience in The House—when she thought she heard Nancy and someone else discussing something in an intensely conspiratorial way.

'Oh . . . oh, I paid her back very quickly,' answered Laura, flustered. 'I sent the money to her in less than a month.'

'That doesn't really answer the question,' said Vixen. Laura stared at her, the hazel eyes wide and panicking. My God, thought Vixen, she's scared of me. Right at this moment, she's scared of me. A curious feeling of power came over her—and she pursued her subject relentlessly.

'Was Nancy your best friend?' she asked.

'Oh no, not at all,' said Laura. 'She was just the only other person I knew in the area apart from my mother.'

'So . . . if she wasn't your best friend and if you hardly ever saw her, how come she lent you money? You must have done something for her.'

'Well . . . well . . . initially I just went there because I knew she ran a boarding house and it would be somewhere to stay for a couple of nights. And . . . and . . . we got talking and she . . . and she . . . '

'Mum,' said Vixen.

'Yes?' said Laura almost in a whisper.

'Has this got anything to do with Douglas?'

There was a dead silence for a moment. Vixen glanced all round the room and saw that they were completely alone there now although she hadn't heard the other people leaving because she had been concentrating so hard. Her eyes found a clock behind the bar and it was quarter to eleven. A quarter of an hour to closing time.

She looked back at her mother and had the shock of her life. She was looking at something she had never thought to see: her mother was crying.

'He's . . . my brother, isn't he?' said Vixen, stunning herself with her own words. Surely the ceiling had to crash in now . . .

'Yes.'

'And . . . and . . . is he Dad's son?'

'Yes! I must have got pregnant just before I left him. But I didn't know till I got here. I didn't know what else to do! I couldn't go back . . . and Nancy was desperate for a child! . . . and . . . and she knew that story about the other baby . . . '

118

Laura put her head down on the table and howled.

Vixen was speechless now. She plucked at her mother's sleeve a couple of times but got no response. For once in her life, Laura was completely out of control.

But not for long.

The next thing Vixen knew was the doctor standing in front of them—breathless as if he had been running.

'Come at once,' he said. 'I had trouble locating you. I'm sorry to be so alarming but I suggest you run.'

And that was how they left the pub, the three of them at a run; Vixen way in front, her mother keeping a good pace behind, and the doctor struggling a long way behind her.

At five to eleven, they were dashing into Alice's house. Vixen dropped back at this point and her mother ran past her into the parlour. She saw her bend down by Alice's sofa and, in a sudden fit of shyness, she herself bent down, still in the hallway, to fiddle with a shoe. And because of the lace that didn't need doing up, she was a minute too late for the death of a grandmother to whom she had only just been introduced.

Eighteen

It was dawn now. There were hundreds of things in Vixen's head, like a pack of hounds—so there was nothing she could do but run.

Her feet were questing through the first field. It was very dry ground and cracked like china. She was running along the edge of a wheat crop and occasionally a pale, bent head of it would fall across her shins. Ruts threatened to trip her every now and then but she managed to skirt them—being chased all the time by the dogs, the questions:

What will happen? What will happen? Will it all stay a secret—only with herself included as well now? Or will Laura tell Kevin? She ought to: Douglas is his son. And Douglas? He should know who his real relations are. Or should he? Maybe he's better off being left as he is. And what about Nancy? She would go mad if she didn't have Douglas any more: he is her life. Or could Nancy and Kevin get on? Could they possibly get together? Or would Laura and Kevin get back together? And would Douglas have to live with his own parents anyway even if the secret was out? Who says a whole family has to live together? They could all just visit each other. But would Nancy be jealous? She might hate to share Douglas. And what about the law? Would Nancy and Laura be 'done' for what they did?

All these thoughts were barking at her on and on and she suddenly realized she had already done several fields and for some reason, she was veering away from the wood. She didn't pause for a moment but doubled back on herself and made for the blue-ish edge of the trees. The sun was climbing higher and some of the birds were so loud they were almost screaming. Vixen ran right round the wood. And still she didn't stop. She ran in a different direction across a field until she came to a pond. Round and round the pond she went several times. There was one solitary duck on it and he was regarding her with gravity and that expression reminded her of Douglas. She spun away from the pond, tears piercing her eyes, and started to zigzag. This was the longest run she had ever done. She was starting to go light-headed with exhaustion. Did this mean the hounds had left off for now? Had she outrun them? Would she be able to stop though? Would that mean that they'd catch up with her again?

Her eyes were clouding over: she had to blink violently to clear them—and still she was going zigzag across a mass of field-land. It's too much, she wanted to cry. Too much for me on my own! Suddenly, just as she was reaching a large-ish bush, a fox, a real one, darted out in front of her. She nearly cried out in relief and delight. She could have sworn that it turned its head and grinned at her, tongue hanging out, eyes glittering—the way animals do. And then it ran. It was taking over from her. She could stop now. She flung herself on the ground and everything went black for a few seconds.

When she came to, the light was dazzling. She shielded her eyes with her hand—and saw two figures walking towards her like celestial creatures because both of them seemed to be in white. This reminded her of the first time she had met Douglas which unnerved her a lot and made her want to cry again. But as the figures got nearer, she realized that they were people, not angels, and only one of them was in white anyway. This was her father, who must have been contacted a few hours ago and was now appearing in his baggy white shorts and T-shirt. The other person was her mother. Vixen watched with awe as they walked towards her. It was years since she had seen the two of them both at the same time. They weren't touching each other but they were walking at the same pace and wearing very similar boots— although they were neatly polished and tied with flourishes on her father's feet; and worn and scuffed from a thousand different places on her mother's.

Vixen just waited.

Was Douglas on his way too? And Nancy? Sandals, not boots, in each of their cases.

She waited some more.

Also by Frankie Calvert

The Sea Serpent
ISBN 0 19 271739 1

There was something very strange about Serpenton. It felt lost somehow—as if half of it wasn't really there. As if it was waiting for something . . .

Fourteen-year-old Helena reluctantly goes to spend the summer holidays in Serpenton, a remote seaside village, to help look after seven-year-old Trevor. While there, she becomes involved with the local amateur dramatic company who beg her to play the leading part in a play about a local legend, the sea serpent. Helena is delighted, but soon she begins to notice something odd about the company: the little boxes they all wear slung over their shoulders; their old-fashioned clothes—and, strangest of all, the fact that no one else can see them.

And then she learns about the bomb that landed on the village in the Second World War . . .

'A well-written, eerie story.'

The School Librarian